THE FINAL INVENTION

The Final Invention

Christian Yeasted

ISBN: 979-8-9899148-0-7 (Paperback) / 979-8-9899148-1-4 (Ebook) / 979-8-9899148-3-8 (Kindle) / 979-8-9899148-2-1 (Audiobook)

Cover design by Gabriel Murillo Nader, 2024.
Author photograph by Renita Yeasted, 2024.

Website: https://authorcyeasted.com

To my dear wife Renita.
And to our four kids, I guess.

Contents

Copyright   iv

Dedication   v

PROLOGUE   ix

1   1

2   4

3   7

4   11

5   17

6   28

7   31

8   38

9   47

10   54

11   61

12   75

viii | Contents

13	82
14	90
15	98
16	106
17	112
18	123
19	128
20	130
21	136
22	145
23	155
24	162
25	173
26	176
27	184
28	186
29	193
30	200
A Note from the Author	205
Acknowledgement	207
About the Author	209

PROLOGUE

Her father told her more than once, "A computer is a tool."

Maybe he was right, but what he had failed to tell her was whether it could become something more.

A vast ocean horizon lay before Elizabeth Foster as she pondered this question. Her father had believed that all technology is created to serve humanity. At first, she accepted these words as truth, but as years passed in a world where computers were becoming smarter by the day, that truth became opinion, and soon it was misinformation. Following her nineteenth birthday, the man who had loved her, fed her and tucked her in every night had passed, and now she kept his words in her mind if only to hear the echo of his voice.

The very first light of the morning sun sent a glistening stream of white over the waves, each peak spreading itself on the shoreline with a gentle hushing as a mother might soothe her child. Cold sand engulfed Elizabeth's feet. Her skin began to bake ever so little under the rising orb, but she welcomed the sensation.

Her fair complexion and prominent cheekbones were inherited from her mother, and if she ever neglected to apply

SPF 50 under a midday sun, her cheeks could become as red hot as branding irons. Her nose was petite but could suffer the same fate in a blinding hot sun, and a full head of auburn hair flowed over her slender neck and shoulders that brandished arms of modest muscle. It was Elizabeth's custom to use the gym as an outlet for daily stress, but today she decided a sunrise on the beach would be the perfect venue for meditation. She closed the lids over her dark brown eyes.

At this moment of serenity, hardly anyone from the local town was out of their homes. Elizabeth reckoned most locals were enjoying a late sleep in their beds, and so she had a clear view of the shore, unobstructed by the daytime beach crowd. As she gazed in wonder at the open scene before her, it seemed she was the only person around, and she had the world all to herself. She drew in a deep, refreshing breath.

But as alone and undisturbed as she felt, the fact remained she was not the only person on this beach. A few other eager beach enthusiasts had arrived even before Elizabeth. They came at dawn to see the same view. They had come to gaze in wonderment at the same sun as it illuminated the same ocean under the very same azure sky. These strangers had spread out over a half mile of shoreline, some strolling slowly along the water's edge and stopping occasionally to pick up seashells or glance at the sunrise, others sitting on their blankets and taking in the whole morning scene. The rays of the sun had warmed their skin even before warming hers, and some of them had even put in a several mile run before ending up on the shore for some well-deserved cooldown stretches. A few of them walked across her field of vision. Their silhouettes seemed to create tiny stains on the otherwise perfect panoramic picture of sand, water, and sky.

But she would not allow herself to be bothered by them. She closed her eyes again and let the continual shushing of the ocean fill her ears. Even though there were others now in her world, to Elizabeth the environment was no less beautiful.

When her eyes opened, they casually turned to her left and then right. Up and down the coastline a different side of early morning beach life revealed itself. Where the sand was damp and flattened the shore was riddled with hundreds of tiny holes. Around each hole was a thin pile of sand as if some burrowing animal had made a quick attempt to get underground and had not bothered to hide its escape route. Elizabeth peered a little closer. A shadow the size of a quarter floated up from the water toward the holes. Then it disappeared. Another shadow, and another, and as they moved with speed up the sandy incline, Elizabeth recognized the miniature camouflaged crabs just above their shadows. Hundreds of sand crabs had been out foraging overnight, dominating the seashore, and making it their playground. But with the rising of the sun the hundreds of crabs had to scurry back into their burrows to take shelter from the elements and from predators. She watched the last crab scuttle out of sight. Then the sand lay still, and she turned her attention back to the horizon.

Soon something else moved into Elizabeth's line of sight. As it scuttled toward her from several feet away, she noticed this crab was alone. All the other crabs were a good 50 feet down the shore. Unlike the others who were heading back into their holes as crabs typically do, this one seemed to have a different agenda. Elizabeth stood watching it in mild curiosity as it came in her direction. Normally, she thought, a tiny life form such as this would know to steer clear of a much bigger creature like her. Yet it drew even closer, and she decided to give the crab a friendly reminder that it was heading in the wrong direction. With the top of her foot, she gently flung some sand at the miniature crustacean. The sand fell all around it and onto it, but despite her direct hit the crab continued toward Elizabeth undeterred. It scurried fast to within inches of her ankles, and she was certainly amused by the tenacity of this little crawler. She figured the crab had a mission in mind and was bent on seeing it through. With a smile and some admiration, she decided to allow the crab to go about its mission whatever that may be, and for the first time since the sun had risen, she lifted her feet from the sand and stepped to her left. In this instance the crustacean deserved much credit. After all, it's not every day that a small lifeform causes a much larger lifeform to move.

1

Early Saturday morning, crowds of tourists flowed out of the hotel elevators to gather in the lobby for the big event. Metal doors slid open on either side of the hall, and families with children of all ages emerged to join the congregation. A few adults had awoken mere minutes ago, with bags under their half open eyes and scraggly hair thrown into buns. The children, however, had clearly been awake for longer. The little ones tugged their parents' arms forward as they jumped in excitement at what lay in store that day.

While she may not have had quite the enthusiasm of a child about the day's main event, Elizabeth was eager to proceed to the viewing site. Most of the people had arrived at the hotel two days ago. After picking up their passes they sat for a tutorial on what to expect from the coming Saturday. The event coordinators animated the audience with descriptions of the upcoming spectacle in such detail that the listeners could picture themselves there already.

Now the big day had finally arrived. Elizabeth smiled as she placed the visitor pass around her neck. She lifted her hair over the lanyard. The nylon threads that brushed her skin conjured a memory of her father who, in his gentle way, laid a similar lanyard around her head many years ago. Young Elizabeth bunched her hair in a ponytail and flipped it over the nylon band, lifted the visitor pass to eye level, and admired it as if she were holding a precious, irreplaceable photograph. Her dad placed a hand on her shoulder, and when their eyes met, he smiled, accentuating some of his wrinkles.

The memory of those happy times dissolved as another tourist grazed past her. Elizabeth moved further into the crowd. She made her way to the front where the event coordinator was shouting above the tumult of voices, "Just five minutes, folks, and then the next shuttle comes." Elizabeth glanced down at her phone to check the time, then with a swipe of her thumb she accessed her messages. A new one from work, one from her friend Sebastian, and one from Teresa, her roommate and lifelong confidant. She smirked at Teresa's amusing text which read, "I wish I could share your excitement right now, but I don't." No doubt at this very moment, thought Elizabeth, her roommate must be keeping herself busy. One of the things Elizabeth had always admired about Teresa was her unceasing work ethic, and she never complained, nor was she ever bothered by how seemingly insurmountable the workload was. No matter how great the obstacles ahead, Teresa had shown unwavering resolve to roll up her proverbial sleeves and get the job done. And a truer friend there never was. As Elizabeth saw it, throughout history there has been only a handful of people who, by their steadfast principles and uncompromising loyalty, could be called truly trustworthy. And her friend was one such individual. Plus she made Elizabeth laugh.

Before long the coordinator bellowed, "Two minutes, folks! Please have your passes ready so you can board the shuttle." Elizabeth closed out of her phone and slid it back into her pocket. She felt it vibrate and thought, *Probably from work, considering how many emails I get every day, every hour,* but this time she resisted the urge to check, attending instead to the noteworthy events unfolding around her. She focused on the hum of voices in the crowd. Lifting her eyes toward the glass doors in front of her she took note of the scattered clouds in the otherwise blue sky, and the trees sat perfectly still to show the absence of any breeze. The forecast was for partly sunny skies and a heat that felt like 94 degrees Fahrenheit. The hot air currents were rippling off the cars that sat idling in the lot outside. Then the faint sound of an engine grew steadily louder, and soon a large shuttle bus came to a stop in front of the glass doors. "OK, everyone," the coordinator announced, "Please scan your pass at the shuttle entrance when you get on board. Enjoy the drive, and then have a great time!" Elizabeth inched forward with the others as the crowd made its way out of the hotel lobby and into the sun. She aligned with everyone into a single file line, or the closest thing to it with children bouncing around, then she swiped her pass and sat down in the air-conditioned bus. When all the seats were filled and the door to the vehicle closed, she breathed in relief, while the remaining people outside her window waited in the heat for the next shuttle. The faint growl of the engine grew louder as the shuttle rolled forward. Then it headed out of the parking lot and made its way to the viewing site for the rocket launch.

2

In another part of town, in a room that had been vacated for the weekend, through windows with blinds drawn there shone the faint morning light from the street outside. The soft gleam fell upon a solitary desk with a computer, its screen black and lifeless. A few dust particles floated aimlessly in the dim stream of sun. All at once the black of the computer monitor illuminated, and the logo of the operating system appeared for a few seconds before being replaced by the main page. Then the Internet home page filled the screen, and soon a line of videos was scrolling up the monitor in single file. One of the videos opened to show a dramatic scene of a young couple quarreling until it escalated to screaming. As the events unfolded in that clip, another video opened to a park filled with children laughing as they played on the jungle gym, seesaw and swings. A third video opened to reveal a mother reuniting with her son after he had gone missing, and still another window enlarged to show a teenager coaxed by his friends to eat something disagreeable on a dare. In one broadcast people reacted to other people's videos, while in another, people displayed their emotion at receiving handfuls of cash. The line of video clips scrolled up the computer screen, and soon dozens of windows were playing their content, voices and sound effects and music overlapping and vying for the viewer's attention.

This continued for some time. The constant influx of new footage brought demonstrations of what seemed the most random activities. Kids smiling while riding their bicycles. Adults sobbing over the loss of a cherished friend at the funeral. An exuberant screech from someone bungee jumping off a platform, and the anger of a man who discovered his drone had been shot down by his next-door neighbor.

Perhaps what happened next was inevitable. A video enlarged and began to play footage of two men talking about a subject in which they were both invested. As the conversation ensued, one of them leaned closer and spoke more clearly and with more intention, while the other leaned closer still and quickly raised his voice in intimidation, jabbing his finger in the air near his opponent's face. Occasional spittle flew from his mouth as he roared without reserve. The closer he got to the other man the more threatened the man became. Then the yeller jolted backward, the other man shoving him hard. The yeller paused for a split second. His pupils dilated. His retaliation was swift. He shoved back, and in an instant the two men locked bodies and grappled to the ground. It did not take long for yeller to gain his position overtop the other, and his hands moved to the throat of his victim. They remained there until all life drained from the man's eyes.

Countless other windows appeared on the computer monitor. Soon the screen was a collage in motion with hundreds of movies streaming, legions of people doing things that people do. Boys and girls, men and women were talking, laughing, crying, and screaming. They were walking or running, driving or standing, dancing or clumsily falling, embracing or bludgeoning. Some of the clips were appropriate for children. Some were violent and horrifying. But in the cacophony of sounds and images, a history of human interaction unfolded in all its glory and its shame.

Then, as quickly as they had first appeared, the movie windows all closed. The webpage disappeared. The home screen went black, and the computer monitor once again sat still in the faint light that penetrated the window blinds. At last, all was quiet.

3

The shuttle bus drove Eastbound for the coast. It would soon rendezvous with a ferry which would then proceed on an eight-hour journey to the famous viewing site. Sitting in her seat and peering out of the window, Elizabeth couldn't help overhearing a few bits of conversation from the others in her group who bellowed with excitement, "They say it's supposed to be one big party on the way there," and, "I wonder how far the launch site is from the mainland."

"The guy with the microphone said it's over 200 miles away," responded another. "It's gonna take all day to get there."

"Yeah, but what a way to travel. Unlimited movies and arcade games," said the first, counting with his fingers, "all-you-can-eat buffets, and nothing but top shelf."

As the bus came to its final stop at the port, everyone in the vehicle peered through the nearest window at the ferry sitting motionless in the tranquil water. The ship was an immaculate white, and its outer hull seemed to shine as if the entire vessel were fluorescent. When the bus hissed to a stop, all the passengers shot up from their seats, grabbed their bags, and exited through the automatic folding door. While people fumbled in their pockets to pull out their ferry passes, Elizabeth already had hers in hand, and she moved ahead of the crowd across the concrete until she reached the bottom of the ferry ramp. There she presented her pass once again, marched up the ramp and proceeded to her designated cabin.

It was a tiny room, but cozy and well maintained. The bed was neatly made with bright white sheets over fluffy pillows, and the tiled floor panels glistened from the recent sweeping and mopping, compliments of the robot tucked away in the charging station under the armoire. She set her bag on the only chair in the room and then sank into the supple mattress for a moment of rest. On the end table was a welcome packet she opened to find a map of the ferry layout. "Perfect," she thought, and without further delay she arose and started exploring, as was her custom. Curiosity compelled her to tour every square meter of the vessel. As she walked about the deck, observing each detail, she filed it away in her vast database of knowledge that her friends called "trivia". Once satisfied she had learned everything worth knowing on the ship, she returned to her room to do some work.

Hours passed. Elizabeth stayed mostly on her computer and phone, accessing ongoing construction projects and communicating with friends and colleagues. She did, however, make it a point to step out of her room frequently and take in the salty breeze from the ocean that sparkled in the sunlight. Occasionally she stopped off at the commissary for a sampling of seafood, and on the last round she complemented the oysters with a generous glass of Riesling. People walking along the deck smiled at her as she made her way back to the room, and she returned their pleasantries with a friendly "how's it going".

In her cabin she worked throughout the day until her phone alarm signaled it was time to walk over and join the gathering throng of onlookers portside. She rose from her chair and stretched her arms toward the ceiling. Walking along the deck she passed the flashing lights of the arcade and the muffled electronic dance hall beats.

A din of excited voices grew louder as she approached. The people in the crowd were all facing the same direction, peering out over the edge of the ferry to watch the glistening spectacle on the ocean's horizon. On a distant floating platform, there stood an upright whitish chrome tower gleaming in the bright sunlight. The booming voice of an event coordinator sounded overhead, reminding everyone they can get a closeup view on the giant TV screen next to them. A few heads turned to the video of a static camera zoomed in on a solitary object, a rocket, poised upright and pointing to the atmosphere. "Just five minutes left before takeoff, everyone!"

The image of the rocket destined for the stars summoned a keen memory for Elizabeth. She had been to a rocket launch once before. Her family had taken her to this monumental achievement of humanity as it rose through the clouds before breaking free of Earth's gravity and forging the long journey to Mars. There had been nothing particularly important about the launch. That trip to the red planet was routine, if such a word can be used to describe the engineering marvel of spaceflight. Yet she could still recall the feeling of pride she had in her fellow men and women, those who had answered the call to bring humanity out of its mundane tradition and take charge of its future.

The countdown timer reaching two minutes on the TV roused her from the nostalgia. Scorching sunlight irradiated the audience on the deck as beads of sweat formed on their foreheads and in their hair. A robotic attendant was passing around ice cold water bottles. Elizabeth put her hands on the safety railing around the ship and leaned over the waves, the warm metal heating her palms. Soft breezes from the ocean gently coursed through her hair and cooled her face, and she gazed across the water at the spacecraft shimmering on the platform, dimmed only by the occasional cloud casting its shadow. Then the voice of the event coordinator resounded, "Alright, people, one minute left until takeoff! The countdown will start at T minus 10 seconds."

With the short time remaining, Elizabeth sent a picture message of the rocket to some of her closest friends. She quickly put the phone away before any response came, and as she did the countdown began. "T minus 10...9...8..." the voice echoed in a methodical tone. "7...6...5...4...". Some onlookers leaned as close as they could toward the horizon, their eyes occasionally twitching up to the large TV livestream, while others had binoculars or stood with phone in hand and camera zoomed. Elizabeth tightened her grip on the railing. "3...2...1...lift off."

4

It was a clear, crisp morning back in town as the citizens walked up the main street sidewalk. Some were at a brisk pace on their way to work or on their morning errands, while several individuals strolled along the sidewalk as they headed for a coffee shop. Others were making their way to the gym. Within the crowd were the latest fashion of trim work suits, and a few well-dressed businessmen and women darted around ladies carrying yoga mats or couples interlocking hands.

A number of people on the sidewalk had their personal robotic assistants with them. Most of the newer models were biped or quadruped, as the wheeled assistants tended to be less agile and take up more space. One model was carrying large shopping bags stuffed with groceries and with clothing bunched together over hangers. The image was something like a donkey lugging around saddle bags while balancing on its hind legs. Another assistant, a less expensive model, was merely a box mounted on a pair of legs, and its ostrich-like extremities pranced along the outer edge of the sidewalk, keeping pace for a human male running close behind as he panted for breath.

The windows of most buildings bordering main street displayed videos of ordinary people jogging, swimming, walking their dogs or lifting light weights. There might be a group of elderly ladies doing chair yoga, a single nonagenarian with a walker making her way through the park, or an obese but attractive young man at the edge of an Olympic size pool convincing himself to go for a lap, but no matter who was featured, the same message weaved through each display: get your work out, get energized, save on medical costs, be happier, and get paid for each successful week of exercise.

There among the throng of people dressed in colorful attire was a gentleman of middle age. His shabby brown hair was heavily peppered with gray, and his weather-beaten face bore the many wrinkles of too much partying in younger years. Despite the name on his birth certificate reading Nicholas, his mother had called him Nico and was the only one who ever had. When she fell ill, he sacrificed his social life to be her sole caregiver for many years until now, after her passing, the only people who called him anything had to first ask him his name.

Quite contrary to the louder modern fashions, Nicholas wore a hodgepodge of throwback clothes from the local thrift store. He had black sweatpants with elastic at the ankles, a T-shirt bearing more than a few holes, and a jean jacket to cover them. He completed this anachronism with a baseball cap, on the front of which was a logo of his favorite team who long ago had been the champions of their division but now had outlived their glory days. Nicholas could relate to this. As a river of people flowed around him, bearing outfits of outrageous neon rainbow elastic, Nicholas felt like a speck of dirt within a kaleidoscope.

He had been down on his luck for years. He had trouble getting a job. Long ago his car had broken down, and he couldn't afford a new one. His arthritis kept him up at night. He had no woman and nobody to call a true friend. The electricity in his apartment had just been turned off due to lack of payment, and when he filed a complaint with his landlord it escalated to an argument that put Nicholas out on the street looking for a new home yet again. Nicholas felt like everything bad that could happen to him did happen. His doctor diagnosed depression, but Nicholas knew it was his terrible luck and the chronic, unrelenting pain in his knees, hips, and hands that dimmed any light at the end of his long, lonely tunnel. Often he wondered why life had not been better to him.

Nicholas continued his arthritic ambling down the street. As he passed by the ATM outside the bank, something strange caught his eye. There, nestled in the basin under the cash dispenser, was a thick stack of pristine 20-dollar bills. He slowed to a halt. His first glance up and down the sidewalk was one of curiosity to see if someone had mistakenly left behind their withdrawal, but then, when nobody claimed this small fortune, Nicholas turned his gaze back to the cash that could be the answer to a lot of his problems. For fear someone else may take it if he didn't move fast enough, it was time to make a quick decision.

His next glance at the people up and down the sidewalk was motivated by a different emotion. Beneath his gray, fraying eyebrows his eyes flickered down to the money, then they shot side to side as he moved toward the ATM. Nicholas had never been one to contain his emotions well, but in as casual a way as possible he reached out and grabbed hold of the stack. Then without looking around he stuffed both of his hands into his pockets and walked away with a plan to circle back soon.

Nicholas looked back over his shoulder at the ATM, and he saw another man now standing in front of it. This could have been a patron of the bank, he thought, but it was peculiar how the man stood staring at the machine without typing anything. The man's furrowed brows lifted as he made a quick glance around him and then again at the ATM. By now Nicholas was familiar with such behavior, as he had acted the same a moment ago, and he knew what would happen next. The man at the ATM coyly placed the cash in his pocket and skulked away with his head to the ground. Nicholas wondered if his own actions at the ATM were just as obvious. He moved quickly back to the machine and saw yet another man standing in front of it without typing a thing. This newcomer also turned his head left and right, but he was gracious enough to ask those around him, "Does this money belong to anyone?"

Nicholas approached fast and said the stack of twenties was his. The newcomer gave him a questioning look, so to convince this gentleman of his integrity and financial stability Nicholas produced the wad of cash he had in his pocket. Nicholas said the automatic teller malfunctioned and gave him only a fraction of what he had ordered for withdrawal. A few passersby noticed this pair of men facing off in front of an ATM, and from their interaction it was clear they were anything but old friends. Nicholas went on to say that he planned on notifying the bank of the malfunction, but now apparently, he wouldn't need to since the ATM was working again.

Regardless of whether he believed Nicholas or not, the gentleman saw no need to question him further and stepped to the side. Nicholas grabbed the cash. As he walked away, he overheard a whisper from some people assembling at the ATM, and their murmur was getting louder despite his growing distance from the scene. There were a few exclamations from those in the crowd, enough for Nicholas to look back and see many more people gathered around the teller machine. His lips parted slightly as he looked in wonder at the automated teller spitting out one stack of cash after another. The bills overflowed the money basin and began to drop, floating and fluttering down to an ever-growing pile in front of the machine. Without further pause, one onlooker bent over and scooped up as many bills as his two hands could grasp. A woman on the other side of the pile mimicked these movements, and then into the green paper mound dove the others in the crowd.

Soon people were trying to muscle their way through the dense blockade of bodies, frantically grasping and clawing at the money being dispensed from the winning slot machine. There was more shoving and even more shouting, arms and legs flailing about in what was now a mosh pit. Many on the outside of the semicircle stood frozen in amazement at the violent spectacle before them, until all at once their heads turned in the same direction toward a blaring siren.

Police cars came up quickly and illuminated the scene with flashes of blue and red. Given his streak of bad luck lately, Nicholas decided to remove himself before any more misfortunes could befall him. He walked away, again as casually as he could, but this time with his lips curled in a smile fueled by avarice.

5

Sitting in a self-driving rickshaw, Elizabeth watched the buildings of her hometown move by one spire after another reflecting across the outer glass of her vehicle. *Feels good to be back,* she thought. *In fact, it's good just to be on dry land.* Despite her lack of enthusiasm for the sea, the rocket launch had already taken its place among her more cherished memories.

As the car continued toward Elizabeth's destination, grocery stores, business offices, restaurants, tech shops and clothing boutiques flaunted their giant advertisement screens and holograms to entice anyone who had taste and a wallet. The vehicle slowed as it approached a kiosk opposite the sidewalk. With her payment already extracted through her phone, she exited the vehicle without a word and walked up to a table jutting from the front of a red brick building. On the table was a large cube colored in burgundy sheen. The bottom half of the cube had an opening where a small mechanical arm held an even smaller black tube, suspended like a single incisor in a jack-o-lantern mouth. Elizabeth sat on the bench and slid up to the table. She placed her hands in the opening, and a soft strap closed over her thumbs. The tube spread nail polish over her fingernails with precision. When the straps released, she walked farther up the street as the polish dried, and soon she arrived at a place she frequented almost daily.

Above her was the cursive sign for a coffee and espresso bar called The Agora. She loved this place not only for its variety of coffee selections and bold flavors, but also for the company it kept. Nearly every morning before work she gathered with her friends Sebastian and Xavier at this aromatic shed nestled among the gleaming skyscrapers of her fair city. Her friends would talk about their day and maybe share some jokes while commenting on the latest shows. But what she loved most about this coffeehouse was how it served as an arena for intellectual debate among her friends. Sebastian Hill worked as a physician. Xavier Bojovnik was a history teacher, but prior to that he had been a sergeant, earning his stripes through numerous muscle wrenching, hunger provoking and sleep depriving trials in the military. Both men brought a great deal to the table for intelligent discussion, and Elizabeth's background in robotic engineering and computer programming were a complement to her friends' knowledge.

As she neared The Agora her phone buzzed. She swiped her thumb over the screen to answer. "Hey, Sebastian. I'm here." Sebastian's crystal clear and pleasant voice responded they were at their usual spot. When she got out of the car the aroma immediately wafted into her sunburnt nose. She was eager to try out a new blend of coffee and whatever else the baristas saw fit to add. Elizabeth had learned to trust the judgment of the employees at this coffee shop. They were creative and knew her taste well, and to this day she was never disappointed in their selection. Upon entering she saw two men sitting across from each other at a table in the corner. They stood and greeted her as she approached.

To her left was Sebastian, a gentleman six feet in height who readily displayed his warm smile within his thick, well-groomed beard of coal black. He had a rare combination of blue eyes to complement the black waves atop his head, and his pale skin made these features all the more vivid. To her right was Xavier, much taller with a thicker frame. It was the policy of this man to dress impeccably. His short cut of brown hair was maintained close to his scalp, a custom from his former career, and he was clean shaven at all times with a hint of tan to his skin. His eyes were a much darker shade, nearly the color of midnight, but despite his somewhat intimidating appearance he was regarded as a large teddy bear by nearly all who met him. Xavier pulled the chair out for Elizabeth to sit while Sebastian asked how her trip went, to which she gave a concise story, painting a colorful picture of the last 24 hours.

"Sounds nice," Xavier said with a face that revealed his lack of interest in space exploration. "Why didn't you just take Sebastian's boat?"

"You're pretty free with other people's possessions, eh, Sarg?"

"You hardly use it," said Xavier.

"And we all know it's technically a yacht," Elizabeth said with a grin.

"Anyway, I wanted the experience of watching it with a crowd, like last time. Also," she added with a raised eyebrow wrinkling her forehead, "I don't have a boating license."

The waitress set a black coffee down in front of Xavier and a double shot of espresso near Sebastian, a ribbon of steam and burnt aroma rising from the tiny porcelain demitasse. Elizabeth placed her order and thanked the waitress who went back behind the counter to prepare a fresh concoction. The friends exchanged some pleasantries about work and life, and the waitress returned with the order, a French pressed blend of Italian and Costa Rican coffee spiced with peppercorns from Senegal. Elizabeth looked down in delight at what lay before her. After a short while she took her first sip, the dark java seeping through her pursed lips and the enriched bold flavor reminding her why The Agora was at the top of her list.

While Sebastian and Elizabeth continued their discussion of space flight, Xavier ran his thumb over his phone until an article caught his attention.

"Hm, another local hospital purchased an AI to help doctors diagnose. Looks like you're one step closer to being jobless, Sebastian. Next comes selling yourself on the street for a nickel."

"Hey, Xavier, be nice," said Elizabeth. "He's worth at least ten cents. But tell me, Sebastian, with AI diagnosing as well as doctors now, how will you support yourself on the street at a dime a trick?"

Sebastian smiled to acknowledge the joke at his expense. "You really think a machine can do a physician's job better than I can?"

"Definitely better than you," added Xavier without batting an eye, "but I think she meant better than humans in general."

"Well there's a few reasons why machines still haven't replaced doctors and probably never will. First, let's be clear, people have been saying machines will replace our jobs since the 19th century at least. Instead the human unemployment rate keeps dropping."

Xavier nodded. "Sure. More jobs to maintain the tech. Career choices increase as society gets more complex."

Sebastian continued. "And through it all, the higher-level education jobs have remained secure.

"Second, when patients tell their problems to a doctor, they're not just feeding the doctor a data set of information. People aren't some technical problem or a mathematical equation to be solved. Patients want to know they're being cared for. They want their physical, emotional, and mental needs addressed."

Elizabeth raised a discerning eyebrow. "Aren't emotions just hormones, serotonin and other chemicals causing our autonomic nervous system to react? What if we're just a bunch of working gears put together to make a walking, talking clock, sophisticated yet predictable? Maybe it just takes a mind more advanced than a human's to understand how all those gears work. Give an AI enough data and it can understand anything, so couldn't it learn the cause of the patient's suffering and the best treatment for it?"

Sebastian shook his head. "The AI can provide a diagnosis, maybe suggest a treatment, but it wouldn't care about how much the patient has to pay out of pocket for the treatment. It couldn't comprehend the loneliness of a patient who has no support from friends or family. It can't even understand the human urge to smoke, drink or overeat since AI has no vices. Name a human ailment, and the bots have never experienced it."

"You've never had Parkinson's," Xavier said, "but you can still treat it."

"Right," Elizabeth said. "Bots may not get sick, but if they can detect our sickness and treat it appropriately, isn't that enough? And they may not have emotion, but they have a very good emotional quotient for spotting sadness or anxiety."

"Look, humans and bots are just wired too differently," said the doctor. "Patients need an empathetic ear, but all they'll get from AI is a bunch of circuits that can't appreciate what it's like to have a frail human body. A machine can't feel the muscle aches or fatigue of someone undergoing chemo. It can't understand depression or the burden of caring for a loved one who's clinging to life as cancer takes hold."

Sebastian paused for a brief moment and looked down while his friends patiently waited, as they did any time the conversation landed on this topic. Elizabeth and Xavier sat in silence and observed their friend while he took in a deep breath, and after exhaling, muttered a one-word apology. He gathered himself and said, "In the end, some human problems need a human touch."

"Human caregivers can be hard to come by," Xavier said. "Nursing homes need bots for lifting the residents, guiding their physical therapy and giving them companionship."

"And family bots can do even more than that," Elizabeth said, incurring the expected eye roll from her friends at this familiar claim. "They help old people get out of their chairs or beds, arrange their medications, help them cook, do the dusting, vacuuming, laundry, scheduling, food ordering, groceries, being your exercise buddy." She paused to reflect for a second and finished with, "Helping to raise your children."

"Listening without end to our verbal diarrhea," Xavier said.

"As much as we can spew at 'em. They'll take it all and never complain." Elizabeth had been guilty of ranting about her day to a family bot from time to time. "And why not," she asked. "It's one of the ways they're marketed: as a life coach. So who cares if machines lack emotion so long as they can fulfill our emotional needs?"

Sebastian leaned forward, intent on proving his point. "If you're hurting, and your girlfriend hugs you, you know she might also benefit from that physical connection. But when a robot hugs you, it feels nothing. It doesn't need your affection and won't reciprocate it. The machine can't lower itself to join in your joy or misery, it just hugs you because it's programmed to."

"Which makes you a charity case," Xavier said, his voice echoing inside his coffee mug as he winked to Elizabeth.

Defending herself against her Luddite friends, she said, "Hey, at least they're consistent. Some people like how a machine's personality and appearance stay the same over time. There's the old saying 'people don't change', but that's not true. Put us in a different environment and in a different crowd and we'll evolve over time. We change our minds unexpectedly. We're erratic. And we age, often becoming a burden."

Sebastian said, "That's part of the pain and the excitement of being human and having human relationships."

"Well I like having someone around whose opinions are a bit more predictable, who's always reliable for a joke, doesn't get moody, and will never grow old or sick. I guess I'm just an old-fashioned gal."

"Ok, but it's different in the medical field. If you strip away the human interaction of something as personal as medical care, then you are devaluing the sense of compassion that people need." "Radiologists," Xavier said. "They don't interact with patients. Where's the compassion there?"

"Compassion is what motivates Radiologists and Pathologists. They know they're not just looking at pictures, but at fellow human beings. Plus Radiologists coordinate when to image, the best imaging to get, and how to limit patient exposure to radiation and IV contrast. The Radiology staff greets the patient and provides the human touch of comfort and reassurance. And when the Radiologists read the image, they understand better than AI what information to provide the doctors in the office. This is all driven by their compassion for patients." Sebastian grabbed his cup, scraping it off the table and sipping the last drop of espresso.

Elizabeth said, "I admit there could be a couple problems with fully autonomous AI doctors. For one, is there any intelligent machine that's free of bias? If one were to diagnose you, you should ask where it was developed. Who was it developed on, and how representative is that population to me as a person? But here's the really big question," she said, leaning forward for dramatic effect, her elbows grinding into the table, "Whom can you sue when something goes wrong? The robot? The health care system? Or does the software company take legal responsibility?"

"First you have to give the AI doctor personhood and full legal rights," Xavier said, "then you sue him."

The doctor rolled his eyes again, nearing his record number of ocular rotations in one morning. "You guys scare me with how far ahead you're planning this."

Xavier offered a historical perspective. "Joking aside, humans will stay responsible for humans. No matter how automated the workplace has gotten and leisure time has increased, humans still go to work every day. You know why?"

"To make money," asked Sebastian.

"To better ourselves and the rest of humanity," asked Elizabeth.

"Because we love water coolers?"

Unmoved, Xavier said, "Because we'll always have problems. Resource consumption, sickness and aging, social inequality and oppression. We'll always work to solve these, even if it means missing some vacation time. No one else, animal or machine, cares as much about our problems as we do, so ultimate responsibility falls to us."

Elizabeth cocked her head to the side in brief consideration, then said, "You know why else we'll always need humans? What's that age old saying? 'The best way to solve problems is not by man working alone or machine working alone, but by man and machine working together'?"

"Never heard that one," Xavier's words echoed as he finished his beverage.

"Gandhi said it." Elizabeth imbibed the last of the French press, doing her best to savor the final drop as it ran down the midline of the cup, leaving a few coffee grounds in its trail. She placed a hand on the shoulder of each gentleman, smiled and said, "Well, boys, this was fun." Both men stood up as she arose from her chair, and they said their goodbyes as she made her way toward the exit.

Sebastian gave the sergeant a quick pat on the back and hastened to join her. "I'm about to hop in a sardine can to take me back home," she told him. "Might not be enough room for two whole people in there, but if you wanna snuggle..." Elizabeth leaned jovially into his shoulder.

"Before you do, how about we walk for a bit," countered Sebastian. "You need to get your land legs back." She acquiesced, and together they meandered down the side of the road, warming their skin in the bright Sunday morning. "I didn't get to compliment you on your dress. Very elegant," he said, keeping his gaze on the sidewalk.

She was well aware of how hard that was for him to say, as only Sebastian's friends knew his struggle. For months he had been drowning in the darkest ocean depths. Every day he rose a little closer to the surface, but only inches at a time. The sun was invisible, the moon and stars beyond reach, air in his lungs a distant memory. And his guilt that he should have done more to save the woman under his care was a weight that threatened to drag him to the ocean floor. His friends allowed him to grieve, but when he started missing work and skipping meals and withdrawing to his isolated apartment, they reached their arms in deep and pulled Sebastian to dry land and fresh air. He would not forget their support, but the guilt would always be a part of him. He continued staring at the walkway in front of him "I know you think about her a lot," said Elizabeth. "We all miss her." He nodded, appreciating the sentiment.

They took their time ambling along the side of the road. In his soft voice he said, "I started packing away her things–." From just down the street there was a deafening crash as a splintering of metal and plastic fragments scattered the pavement.

6

Two cars collided head on in the middle of the street. Crumpled metal and shattered glass exploded over both vehicles, the percussive sound waves hitting the sidewalk and pounding through Elizabeth's chest, and she cursed as all her muscles jolted at once. She and Sebastian were stunned. In the following seconds they could do nothing but stare at the devastation. Then, within the rising smoke, a silhouette in the rear of one car slumped over and collapsed on the seat. This lit a fire in the doctor. "I'll be back," he said, and he took off toward the wreckage.

Elizabeth dialed 911. Although every autonomous passenger vehicle released an emergency signal in an accident, people were still encouraged to call.

When Sebastian reached the crumpled car door he lifted the handle, but the center of the door had been dented in, jammed into the doorframe. As his fingers probed the edge of the door for the best grip, a bystander with brawny shoulders and hands chiseled from years of manual labor ran up beside him, and together they pried open the obstruction and grabbed the passenger from the back seat. Their backs strained as they lugged the unconscious 200 pounds onto the pavement. Then Sebastian pressed his fingers to the man's wrist and neck hoping for a pulse. Nothing.

The doctor put all his weight on the man's sternum and started chest compressions. Soon the heat and the force of every working muscle caused sweat to drip from his nose as he plunged down with extended arms. The passenger's eyes were closed, his scalp and arms were painted with lacerations from the collision, and his body jolted under each downward thrust.

Elizabeth joined them. "Drone's on the way," she said, and as if on cue propellers whirred around the corner of a nearby building. A medical drone with four propellers and a bulky, yellow torso came in fast and hovered above the crash site.

It surveyed the scene, sending its findings to an approaching medical rescue team, then it descended to the ground next to Sebastian. Having been trained on using the medical drone in an emergency situation, he didn't bother waiting for it to finish stating instructions. He reached for the main compartment on its body, popped it open and removed the AED leads. Elizabeth grabbed the gauze and tape from the drone's accessory compartment. Sebastian placed the pads on his patient's chest and waited for the drone to analyze the heart rhythm. Sebastian said, "V-tach. Not good." The drone announced, "Shock advised." All three of them stood clear as the AED delivered the shock. But the attempt was unsuccessful, and the doctor resumed chest compressions with firm yet methodical shoves.

Elizabeth squeezed the gauze bandages onto the gashes in the scalp. She grabbed an elastic bandage from the drone and wrapped it around the victim's head. As Sebastian continued the life support, he could feel the sternal bone cracking under the weight of his thumping, but he didn't stop until they were ready to shock again. The AED once more analyzed the rhythm, and the drone advised another shock. A tone of charging voltage hummed ever louder as everyone stood clear. A second shock was delivered. The patient's rhythm fluctuated, then his heartbeat returned to normal.

The deafening whine of an incoming siren drowned out the doctor's reorienting words. He stood aside as the ambulance pulled up, and two EMS personnel hopped out, working fast to stabilize the patient, load him in the ambulance, drive off and disappear around the corner.

Sebastian, Elizabeth, and the other Good Samaritan exchanged their thanks as well as their shock at the complete implausibility of the situation. Elizabeth glanced behind her shoulder at a sight to which she was not accustomed. "Hey guys," she said, jutting her chin toward the sidewalk. A crowd had formed during the spectacle, and countless people were holding their phones with outstretched arms to record the entirety of the crash, the rescue, and the resuscitation. Elizabeth placed a hand on the doctor's arm and leaned her head to his ear. "You could've run a little faster, you know."

7

Elizabeth and Sebastian stayed to give testimony about the crash. They found a bench on the sidewalk and sat in the shade, a cool breeze evaporating the beads of sweat on their foreheads. Their breathing softened to normal. Elizabeth sent a message to Xavier notifying him of the events, and after resting a moment longer, she stretched her arms above her head in parody saying, "Well, sometimes it's nice to have a break from your routine."

Sebastian scoffed, padding his sleeve against the moisture on his brow. "Yeah, patients at the office are usually a little less impaled."

Elizabeth turned silent, her eyes fastening to the rubble. Despite her upright posture, within her chest an overexcited heart was pounding. This was not the typical recovery following an exciting event or a fast run, where the heart rate eases after a few moments. This drumbeat was harsh, getting louder, and reminding Elizabeth of a family condition that made the machinery in her chest different from the average person's.

Years ago, the first time her thorax erupted into a grand

finale of fireworks, she called for her mother, convinced her young life was at its end. On entering the room Mom observed the red face and white, clutching knuckles Elizabeth held over her chest. In a calm, reassuring voice Mom asked her a question or two and, with a soft hand, guided her daughter's fingers over the throbbing pulse in Elizabeth's neck. All the symptoms evaporated. While Elizabeth was jarred from the experience, she did marvel at her mother's power over what seemed almost certainly a lethal condition. On that day her mother showed her that massaging the carotid artery could make the heart resume its normal, steady pace.

Soon after, she was diagnosed with paroxysmal supraventricular tachycardia, where a steady heart rate could erupt without warning into machine gun fire. The doctor advised the best treatment, but the AI of her insurance company ran the numbers and denied Elizabeth the gene therapy that had helped so many others. According to the AI, her condition was non-life threatening and easily treated with some conservative measures. Despite this calculated assessment, the violent wrench of palpitations kept coming without warning, and it could be made even worse by psychological stress. Her chest thumped, her face flushed, her sweat glands oozed, and she scientifically classified the whole experience as "miserable".

Sitting next to her on the bench, Sebastian observed her reddened face and asked if these were her usual symptoms. In response she employed the treatment that had worked so well for her many times before, holding in a deep breath and gently massaging her carotid. Despite his years practicing medicine, Sebastian was impressed every time with her efficiency in treating these episodes.

Elizabeth composed herself, straightening her posture as Xavier approached and ensured his friends were alright. Then he surveyed the scene, and something caught his attention. Amid the shards of metal and plastic and bits of glass strewn about the cars, the two vehicles were facing head-on, their hoods crumpled inward like smashed eggshells. While the first car had one passenger sitting in the back seat, the other had no passenger, nor did it have any driver to take the wheel in case of an emergency. If the passenger in the first car had been sitting in the front, he thought, there might have been a chance for him to grab the wheel and swerve to safety. Instead, the vehicles had decided to steer into each other, and the result was devastating. "The trolley problem," Xavier said, keeping his eyes on the wreckage.

Elizabeth squinted up at him from her bench. "You mean when someone treats the subway like it's their own personal bathroom?"

"It's philosophy 101," he replied with his usual ursine growl.

"Ah," she replied, "you mean when you see a trolley coming down the track about to hit five people, and you could flip a switch to make the trolley go on a second track, but there's a mom and her kid on the second track?"

Xavier nodded. "Hard to make a good choice in a no-win scenario. Even harder for a self-driving car."

"But does the trolley problem really apply to autonomous vehicles," Elizabeth asked. "They use hi def cameras. They use radar and lidar. They can spot an obstacle well over a mile away and avoid it before the no-win scenario ever comes. Doesn't that eliminate the trolley problem altogether?"

"You can't foresee everything," Sebastian said. "Someone or something could always appear on the road with no warning. Accidents still happen," he said with a gesture toward the devastation before them. "It seems wrong to leave all the driving to machines when the real responsibility to keep everyone safe from our vehicle lies with us."

"A responsibility many don't take seriously, like this poor sap in the back seat," Xavier said, pointing his thumb over his shoulder.

"Okay," Elizabeth said, "but what happened today is more rare than winning the lottery. Compared to human drivers, autonomous vehicles almost always save lives. So ask yourself, is it ethical to leave driving to humans when we have a far better option available?" The men said nothing but gazed at the scraps of metal on the street. "Besides, self-driving cars aren't preprogrammed in the way people think. One of the reasons autonomous vehicles are overall better drivers than humans is that each car has the combined knowledge of a million other autonomous vehicles. There's no ethical question about what the car should do in a no-win scenario. It would just do what all the other cars would, and it would do it better than a human because the car doesn't get fatigued or distracted with texting or driving under the influence."

Sebastian said, "No machine values my life as much as I do, so I'm gonna stay behind the wheel, thanks."

Xavier offered one final thought. "If those cars are all interconnected, they can be hacked."

Elizabeth shook her head. "There are so many redundant safeguards in place for each car."

"There are always cracks in the system," he replied.

Sebastian added, "Yeah, in the old days computer nerds couldn't do any real physical harm to anyone, but if they can get control of the vehicle you're in...well you see what happened today."

A police officer walked from his squad car toward the trio.

"Self-driving cars have a sordid past anyway," Xavier said. "Car companies released them to the public before proper testing was done. Human drivers were guinea pigs."

"Could the car manufacturers have adhered to higher standards of testing, like making sure the cars' vision was flawless before putting them on the road for any untrained human driver to use? Perhaps."

The officer stepped onto the sidewalk and greeted the group of friends. In addition to his badge, he was equipped with communicator, body cam, gun holster and strength amplifying body suit standard for all police officers in the field. The suit was bulky and bunched together at the shoulders and elbows, but most officers at the precinct agreed it was fashionable. He readied his digital tablet to record their eyewitness testimony. Elizabeth and Sebastian gave their account, and the officer scribbled. He glanced up at them when he asked for confirmation they had not witnessed the crash with their eyes.

"We heard it and saw what happened afterward," said Elizabeth, shifting her stance a little, "but no, we didn't see the cars collide."

The officer jotted this in his pad. "I appreciate you sticking around," he said as he nodded and turned back toward his car.

Elizabeth spoke up to get his attention before he went out of earshot. "Excuse me, Sir, but don't you think it's odd that not one but two cars strayed from their lanes at just the right time to collide?"

The policeman paused momentarily and surveyed the scene again. Without taking his gaze from the crash site he said, "We see these kind of things from time to time. No car's a hundred percent safe."

Recognizing she was not getting her point across, Elizabeth said, "And they both happened to be vehicles with no one behind the steering wheel, so nobody could take control in case something like this happened."

Now the officer's eyes flickered toward hers long enough to say, "Not everyone follows the car manufacturers recommendations to stay at the wheel." Sebastian knew Elizabeth well enough to see she was flustered, so before she said anything regrettable, he placed a gentle hand on her arm. With this reminder she froze, and the officer wished them a good day before strutting toward his vehicle.

She muttered to her friends, "No way this accident was random." They looked at her with sympathetic eyes but said nothing. "This doesn't bother you guys?"

Xavier replied, "Let the cops handle it. That's their job."

Sebastian added, "It's not worth debating in public with the police. Anyway, you told him what needed to be said."

"Yeah," said Elizabeth, "he seemed really concerned that this whole collision was premeditated."

Xavier's dark eyebrows furrowed, his mahogany eyes

locking onto hers. "What are you saying," he asked. "Someone tried to kill the guy?"

Elizabeth weighed her words carefully. "I'm saying you can't rule it out."

"It's always good to have a wide differential," said Sebastian. "It really was crazy, Xavier. You saw the wreckage. If somebody wanted to kill him, they certainly could do it that way. He almost didn't make it."

"Almost, except he was sitting in the backseat surrounded by cushioning. If somebody wanted to kill him," said the sergeant, "they could have done a better job. Trust me, there are way more effective ways to take a life."

Elizabeth pondered for a moment, then responded, "Unless you don't want to be caught."

8

A self-driving rickshaw separated from a steady stream of traffic and pulled up to the sidewalk, stopping in front of Elizabeth. "Taxi's here. Seeya tomorrow, boys," she said, ducking into the vacant, golf cart size vehicle. She settled in for the trip home.

On her phone the top of her contact list bore the name of her best friend turned roommate. The dial tone sounded for less than a second before the roommate answered in her usual pleasant voice, "Teresa's Tree Chippers. You find 'em, we grind 'em."

Elizabeth cracked a grin and replied, "Hi, I'm on my way."

"Can't wait to see you, girl. How would you like a fresh oven baked cookie to welcome you home?"

More than a little intrigued, Elizabeth said, "Ooo, what kind?"

"You'll see when you get here, silly." Teresa waited for her to hang up, then Elizabeth put away her phone to soak in the vibrant urban life outside her window.

Despite the cramped quarters, auto rickshaws were still the cheapest and fastest way to get around town, and the sheer number of them ensured one would appear almost immediately upon request through the app.

As Elizabeth's vehicle passed by the salon off the main street, a faint "ping" sounded from the map display, and the car made an unexpected right turn and then left. The taxi was not taking the standard way home.

Every rickshaw in the swarm could be redirected around construction or some roadside emergency, Now, acting on the knowledge of a thousand other taxis and traffic controllers, her vehicle found the most efficient route home. It dashed alongside throngs of people on the sidewalk going about their morning affairs. A mother dragged her squirming child by his forearm as they walked away from the candy shop. Three businessmen were laughing at one of their punch lines. A young couple walked with one hand interlocked and a spare hand scrolling through social media pages.

Elizabeth passed by many others on the sidewalk, but one man caught her attention the most. There was a somewhat disheveled appearance to his outdated baseball cap and jean jacket. He walked with his head down and his hands in his pockets, one of which protruded more than the other. Perhaps the most striking detail was the fan of bills peeking out from inside the bulging pocket. Elizabeth made note of the contrast between the man and the sheer excess of cash jutting from him like a turkey's tail feathers, although she resisted judging anything by its cover. She mused, "Hopefully he puts some of that cash toward a hat of a better baseball team." The man and the rest of the people on that sidewalk disappeared behind the red brick of a building corner as the rickshaw continued toward her home.

As she passed by a side avenue off the main drive, red and blue lights reflected off the buildings lining the street. She figured at least two police cars from the way the lights flickered on the brick walls, and she pondered what might have brought them there.

When she arrived at her apartment she slung her overnight bag around her shoulder, walked to the front door, accessed the apartment app and tapped her wearable to the front door. This app not only granted her access, but she also used it to pay the laundry machines, access the gym, and pay utilities and rent. All this could be done while her ancestors would have been rummaging through their purses to find a keychain.

A cheerful voice from the lobby's front desk chimed through her wearable, greeting her in the usual fashion. "Welcome home, Ms. Foster! Hopefully you had a good trip."

"Sure did," she answered, "but it's good to be back on dry land." Another tenant entered behind Elizabeth and was greeted on his wearable in a similar way, but he marched forward without making the slightest response and joined her on the elevator.

When she exited onto her floor, her feet carried her down the hallway while her nimble fingers twitched up, down and across to access the key to her room. With another wave of her wearable beside a door, her domicile unlocked, and she opened the door to the heavenly scent of baked cookie dough, white chocolate and macadamia nut.

Teresa was lifting a tray from the oven, and on it sat the single dessert. She set the tray on the stove top. The joints of Teresa's white fingers clicked ever so softly as she opened her hands to release the cookie tray, and with the faintest whirring of her arms and torso she turned toward Elizabeth. "Welcome home, girlfriend. Here's the good stuff," she said, gesturing to the dessert. "Help yourself. Would you like something to drink with it?"

"What do I need," Elizabeth asked.

"Based on what you've logged the last couple days you're deficient in several vitamins, and you still have about 1,400 calories to consume today. How about a passion fruit spinach smoothie?"

Elizabeth rubbed her palms together and nodded. A soft mechanical buzzing emanated from the joints in Teresa's neck as she shook her head in disapproval. "Ship food, it just can't beat good old fashioned home cooking." The machine preparing the food issued a wink on her digital facial display.

"It sure can't beat yours," Elizabeth replied. "Well, not since you pilfered Mom's recipes, anyway."

"Don't you mean downloaded," asked Teresa, feigning offense for the sake of humor. "Anyway, it's more like she was the master, and I was her journeyman." Elizabeth breathed in the chocolate, buttery aroma with a grin. "So, tell me all about the launch. The whole trip," her roommate requested as she reclined on the couch, "and please don't spare the details." So Elizabeth picked up the cookie, joined her friend on the pristine white sofa, and began nibbling the pastry as she relayed her experience. Teresa assumed a relaxed posture to invite further storytelling from her well-traveled roommate. Bubbling with eagerness to include her friend in the recent experience, Elizabeth wove her tapestry:

A triumphant starship ascended from the platform, the audience gazing in wonder at the vessel scaling every cloud. Several claps joined a rising hum of whispers from the audience as the spacecraft bulleted toward the top of an azure sky. Some people expressed their amazement with a few scattered cheers, but most of the congregation merely stared upward.

Elizabeth glanced around at the faces in the assembly. She had attended a similar launch as a child, and at that time there seemed to be far more applause and shouts of pride from the onlookers. The heat had undoubtedly worn heavily on today's crowd.

A final round of percussing hands trailed off, while in the troposphere the rocket accelerated ever faster, surging upward through the layer of scattered puffs of white, and then all at once it disappeared into the clouds.

The only sound now was indistinct conversation among the passengers. They turned their backs to the ocean and drifted toward the commissary for the post-launch dinner. In the dining area the banquet tables were filled with the usual buffet selections. Mounds of grilled buffalo and woolly mammoth meat nestled beside plates of manatee-chicken hybrid and dodo, the greasy meat chunks reflecting the heat lamps above them as they exuded their mouthwatering aroma. Further down the buffet table the charcuterie platters held all-you-can-eat almas caviar, a hill of translucent gold ball bearings. Then there were giant ruby Roman grapes, apples and pear, and seedless Densuke watermelon that could have been a black bowling ball sliced to reveal deep red flesh. Alongside the fruit section was a haphazard pyramid of white truffles, and they released their earthy scent as they toppled down on one another whenever passengers whisked them up and piled them on their plates. Elizabeth grabbed some fish eggs, dumped them onto miniature tortillas, and scarfed down her caviar tacos.

Afterward there was live entertainment in the dance hall with plenty of drinks and inadequate air conditioning. The prospect of sweating more than she already had in the baking sun did not appeal to Elizabeth. Instead she returned to her room and sprawled out on the bed.

On her phone she read the responses from her friends Sebastian and Xavier and from her roommate Teresa, responses like "have fun" and "don't fall over the side". Then she finished up some last minute work with the Foreman of her project, answered some emails from colleagues and finally put her technology on the nightstand. "Dim the lights to 20 percent please," she requested of the room. As she drifted off to sleep the ferry churned through the waves, making its way back to the mainland.

In the apartment Teresa asked questions when there was a pause in the story. When Elizabeth finished her tale Teresa said, "It sounds so exciting," taking the utmost care to avoid a patronizing tone.

"There were definitely more people at the one you and I went to all those years ago." After a half-hearted attempt to recollect the specifics of that distant memory, Elizabeth asked her friend, "Mind pulling it up?"

Teresa maintained a relaxed posture on the sofa but turned her head to look up toward the enormous screen on the wall. "Get ready for a little trip down memory lane."

On the flat screen appeared a woman in her 50s, a brunette with hazel green eyes and a wide smile. Strands of her hair danced around in an ocean breeze, while the rest of her remained still as she fixed her gaze on the horizon. Her face eclipsed the beaming sun, making her appear as angelic as the holy figures of cathedral murals.

Sitting in her apartment, Elizabeth found herself unprepared for such an intense ache of loneliness, this cavern in her chest that reopened at the sight of the woman she so admired. She managed to unglue her vocal cords and utter a soft creaking of words. "Mom was beautiful."

Then a man's voice, deep but lighthearted in tone, drew the camera's focus. "Hey, Lizzie, put your phone away and come see this." The voice came from a tall, broad-shouldered redhead. He was standing next to Elizabeth's mother, their hands interlocked, each massaging the other's thumb.

Teresa said, "Your dad's right. You spend way too much time with technology." Elizabeth smirked. The camera now focused on a preteen girl walking toward her parents. Her auburn hair was pulled tightly in a ponytail, leaving her many freckles obvious to anyone looking, which in the adolescent's mind was everybody on Earth.

Her father, the cheerful carrot top, said, "Hey, Teresa, take a family photo." He brought his two ladies together inside his wide embrace. "Make sure you get the launch pad in the background please." The trio smiled at Teresa. A faint click, and the video froze into a perfect image of the happy family. A surge of nostalgic emotion swelled in Elizabeth at the appearance of this photograph, and her throat closed again as though a rope were tightening around it. A thin film of tears coated her eyes, but she fought to uphold them.

Teresa analyzed the glistening in her companion's eyes, and a number of subroutines activated. Compassion, where emotion and intention meet, was not codable for machines. Despite this, family bots were capable of empathy, a collection of codable skills, and Teresa had several algorithms prepared for any number of tearful displays. She placed her hand on Elizabeth's. Their grips gently tightened together. Teresa had known her friend for decades, and in that time, Elizabeth had grown quite accustomed to the feel of her friend's hand, the smooth polymer coating overtop exposed rubbery fingers with tiny bumps of transducers at the fingertips. To Elizabeth, it felt natural.

In the video the young girl and her parents stood in obvious anticipation. Across the rippling waves, a rocket towered over its launch pad. Soon came the countdown, and the whole audience shouted in unison, "3...2...1...lift off!" First the flash of the engine's explosion, followed by the chest rattling boom. The vessel arose amid cheers and wailing and woohooing, and in the family bot's footage the growling of the engine ascending into space was drowned out by thundering applause.

"Listen to that uproar," Elizabeth said to her roommate, still in awe as the spectacle unraveled before her once again.

"They certainly had a right to cheer," said Teresa. "At that time the Mars missions were humanity's crowning achievement."

* * *

Elizabeth scrolled through her social media account while her friend cleaned the dinner from the table. A local news story detailed an event from earlier that day, one that occurred very near Elizabeth's home. "Hey, Teresa," she called over to the kitchen, "can you believe I rode right past that ATM that spat out huge amounts of cash today? I could've been rich."

"You could've been hurt. A lot of people were."

Elizabeth thought back to the man with the baseball cap. "At least one of them made out," she said. "But what would cause an ATM to malfunction like that?"

Recognizing Elizabeth was posing the question toward her, she answered, "Mechanical errors, software issues affecting operations, network or communication failures."

"Could it have been hacked," Elizabeth asked.

As her roommate washed the dishes she accessed historical records of physical ATM breaches, remote ATM unlocking and even jackpotting like the episode today. Within seconds she issued her answer. "Yes."

9

The following morning at The Agora, Elizabeth entered upon a heated debate between her two friends sitting in their usual locale. Sebastian was leaning forward an inch or two, his emphatic finger jabs on the mahogany table doing fierce battle with Xavier's eye rolls. As she approached, they ceased their bickering long enough to greet her. "Tell me you two aren't arguing again about whether golf or wrestling is the harder sport. Remember how that ended?"

Sebastian chuckled. "How could we forget the only time it ever came to blows?"

The atmosphere of testosterone thinned enough to lighten the hint of flushing in Xavier's face. "If by blows you mean I had you in a full nelson."

"I let you pin me all those years ago to give you a false sense of security, and it's still working splendidly," Sebastian said, his fingers tapping together in sheer villainy.

"We were talking about whether bots will ever become infantry," the sergeant said.

"And this cave dweller here doesn't think it'll happen. What about you, Elizabeth?"

She turned to the sergeant. "If I say yes, you promise not to put me in a headlock?"

Sebastian spoke fast to reinforce his viewpoint. "Humanoid bots can do almost anything we can, so why not have them do the fighting instead of human soldiers? Why put our lives at risk when you could just send a soldier bot that can be mass produced?"

While Elizabeth placed her order with the barista, Xavier said, "We already have plenty of bird, snake and dog bots in the field keeping our boys safe, but trust me, when all your machines are destroyed, you'll need well trained human soldiers who can function with no tech. Besides, if we send only machines to defeat a rival country, we accomplish nothing. Real victory is about meaningful control. For that you need human infantry interacting with the locals."

Elizabeth joined them, pulling her chair toward the table with a single screech on the polished stone floor. "Couldn't cyber-attacks or economic sanctions establish meaningful control too?"

The sergeant cocked his head in acknowledgement. "We use a multi-pronged approach, but always with soldiers at the ready."

"But wouldn't bots make better tactical decisions than a human soldier in the field who's tired, under stress and prone to error," she asked.

His answer was swift, as if drawn from a holster. "Even if a soldier bot were built perfectly and had no chance of malfunction, humans still need to stay in the loop. Machines should only kill if ordered to by a human."

"How comforting," said the doctor.

"Better than autonomous weapon systems killing without oversight," Xavier said. "The decision to take a life should be left to humans. We understand the value of life more than a bot can."

Elizabeth posed a hypothetical to the sergeant. "Well if bots are ever allowed to kill and join the infantry, could you see yourself feeling any camaraderie with them?"

Xavier processed the question with furrowed brows. "Camaraderie is built on the sacrifices soldiers make for one another. While tech on the battlefield can keep you alive, you shouldn't sacrifice yourself to keep it functioning. That's the opposite of what's intended. Camaraderie wouldn't make sense."

"Okay," followed Sebastian, "maybe machines wouldn't be ideal soldiers, but could they be medics?"

Xavier sat back and sipped his black beverage. A fond memory flashed in his mind, a swell of pride filling his chest as he smacked his lips and touched his porcelain back to the table. "We loved our medic. He made us more confident on the field because we knew he could patch us up and keep us going. Even a brief interaction with him could propel you forward to thrive in the next strenuous situation. That placebo effect was powerful. You worked harder, you pushed yourself longer because you knew he had your back. A machine doesn't project the same compassion or support. You don't walk away from the encounter with as much confidence."

The waitress clinked a cup onto a saucer in front of Elizabeth. It was filled with the result of countless Ethiopian coffee beans crushed to a thick black powder, the potion from which gave her the electricity to conquer her day. Today's concoction had found its way to her all the way from Sidamo province, where coffee was thought to have been discovered. Nestled 2000 meters above sea level in the Ethiopian highlands, the Sidamo region could boast a strictly high grown coffee, meaning lower oxygen, slower growth, and more time for the plant to absorb nutrients from the local soil. The result was a far more vigorous flavor, and Elizabeth enjoyed the heat on her face from the steam as it wafted out of her cup. "So humans, not AI, should make the decision to take another life," she said, moving the cup closer to savor the rich burnt aroma. "But if you predictably pull the trigger based on certain data, and AI controls how that data is collected and analyzed, are you really making the decision or is the computer?"

Xavier gave a quizzical look. "Make sure your recon tech is reliable. It's the nature of modern warfare to put your trust in technology when you can't see the target with your eyes."

"So why not just make sure your soldier bots are reliable," asked Elizabeth.

"It's not worth the risk. Technology fails too often," Xavier said, "and a failure in the field during an armed stand-off could be disastrous. An autonomous weapon system like a soldier bot could misfire and escalate a war."

"Or start one," Sebastian said.

"It gets worse. A truly autonomous weapon whose actions aren't fully understood could cause other countries to build up their defenses. The balance of power, where all countries know each other's capabilities, could be gone. On the contrary, if you 'mass produce' an army of killer bots, you create a new weapon of mass destruction. Other countries will understand that very well, and they may feel even more cornered."

The trio paused for a moment to enjoy their beverages and ponder their discussion. Elizabeth broke the silence. "Then what if we don't mass produce the soldier bots? What if we just build a few for special operations to eliminate high end targets?"

"Assassin bots," came a sarcastic utterance from the doctor, somewhat in disbelief at his friend's suggestion.

Xavier said, "Actually we already do that with drone strikes. But again, those strikes are ordered by humans. If a bot is allowed to do even a single kill on its own, even of a high-end target, you have to look at what principles are being violated. When you deny one person the right to die by a fellow human, you put all of our rights at risk."

"I suppose another question would be," Elizabeth said, "if a bot decided to kill, what kind of kill would it be? A single shot to the head or a brutal dismemberment? How do you keep the bot from violating basic human dignity?

"Perhaps it's not only important that the enemy is killed, but how they're killed," Sebastian said.

"You'd have to make sure the attack falls within the Law of Armed Conflict." The sergeant elaborated. "You limit injury to the enemy to only what's absolutely necessary. You avoid any weapon that causes unnecessary suffering."

The physician expressed his appreciation that the military operated on a similar code of ethics to his. "Sounds like the principle of double effect. Your action has to be good or neutral, your intention has to be for the good effect and not any possible bad outcome, and the good effect has to outweigh the bad effect. Like when we give a pill that may cause side effects, but our intention is to heal, and the action is one of compassion and goodness. But we too have to do our due diligence to minimize any potential harm."

Xavier responded with a nod, while Elizabeth raised another issue. "So who's responsible if an AI commits a war crime? The military? The manufacturer?"

"Depends on how autonomous the AI system is," the burly man next to her answered. "The more control the manufacturers and programmers have over the AI's actions, the more accountable they are."

As was her fashion, she prodded around her friend's argument using inquiries. She found it was the best way to get her comrades to consider their positions without taking offense. "What do you say about the laws of the Geneva Convention? Are they still enough in a world of AI, drones and cyberattacks?"

"You should always apply humanitarian principles where you can, even to machines or cyber warfare. No matter how advanced the technology, we still have to discriminate between civilian and combatant, protected objects versus military objects, clear military advantage versus just collateral damage." Xavier sipped again at his straight black caffeine. "These are human values. I wouldn't trust machines to understand them. What AI can do for the military is provide us with more courses of action, some of which might meet the very highest of our ethical standards.

Sebastian concluded, "It seems more mechanization on the battlefield forces us to think about what aspects of war are truly human. Which actions should be performed by humans, and what can be deferred to AI."

The triumvirate of friends took a brief moment to taste their beverages, listen to the soft coffeehouse music in the background, and smell the charred saccharinity that permeated the air. After discussing their plans for the day, they finished their drinks, bid each other farewell, and proceeded to their places of work. Exiting the comfort of their favorite locale, none of them could have foreseen what the coming days held in store.

10

Elizabeth was employed as project manager at CSR Construction. This company started years ago building residential housing for middle class suburbanites. In more recent years, however, the management had decided to go in a new direction: constructing public housing for people who did not earn enough to afford other living options. Driven by this new mission, Elizabeth helped her company win enough construction bids from local governments to put up a few low-income abodes, each adorned with an array of colorful perennials that bedazzled a walking path meandering around a pleasant, cozy set of rooms. While the residents were quite happy with their lodgings, what helped CSR gain its reputation as one of the largest non-profit construction industries of its time was the intriguing method it used to build the homes.

For each housing complex, Elizabeth first coordinated the automated landscapers to scrape the ground to a level grade, just in time for a towering 3-D printer to roll in on its treads and spread itself into an enormous rectangular box, hollow and several stories tall, centered over the upcoming home.

Then from the printer at the end of a metallic swing arm emerged the liquid concrete polymer. The printer followed an established blueprint for the first, second and third floor inner and outer walls of the domicile, leaving slots for windows, doors, piping, electrical and insulation. Then much smaller 3-D printers lined up on the upper edge of the newly formed wall and began extruding a liquid metal that would harden within seconds. As it solidified, the printers would glide along the material they had just made and then lay down more of the fluid alloy. Up and up moved the printers until they reached the midline of the home, then back down they went until arriving at the opposite wall. The end result was a series of light yet sturdy metal buttresses that formed the skeleton of the roof. Then came the drones. A humming buzz of five or ten drones filled the air as they swooshed in carrying large tiles made from repurposed wood and rubber. With exacting precision the drones laid down each tile, then flew off to gather another. This process could all be done quickly and at very low cost, a fact that enabled CSR to win more bids than its competitors. But Elizabeth's organization did not stop there with its innovation.

The remainder of the housing was composed of all natural and renewable materials like bamboo, and recycled materials such as plastics were used for anything from pipes to window frames to electric. While this was environmentally responsible and served to self-promote the superiority of CSR homes, the biggest promotion for this institution was its use of the AI foreman.

The concept of the AI foreman first gained popularity in the early 2000's. While human laborers have always excelled at perception, awareness, and decision making, their robot counterparts excel at precision and repetitiveness. Working together, man and machine can achieve great productivity, but they often need proper guidance to do so, and for this purpose the AI foreman was created. The CSR AI foreman was a computer program created to oversee construction projects and enhance the performance of the laborers, both robotic and human. It did this by sending a precisely timed series of instructions to the robots via their built-in software and to the humans via their wearables. All the laborers had to do was carry out the instructions. A human worker might receive a signal on his wearable advising her to proceed to bamboo flooring once he has completed window placement, while another worker may be called to assist with installation of the shower and sink. In the meantime another human would be sent to work in tandem with a robotic jigsaw, puppeteering the mechanical arm to cut small areas with precision. The end result was a symphony of computers, robots and humans all working together. While the workers fiddled and harped on complex design problems, the AI conducted their performance. But if the AI foreman was the brain, and the laborers the organs and extremities, then Elizabeth was the food nourishing this whole proverbial body.

As AI Coordinator, Ms. Foster oversaw the performance of both the AI foreman and the workers, acting as liaison between the two. Years of coming home in the afternoon smelling of sweat, pine and polymer, washing the grime off just in time to make it to evening classes where she studied hard and excelled in software and robotic engineering earned her the title and privilege of AI Coordinator, and now she could troubleshoot any problems that arose in her work environment. If the human laborers needed clarification on directions they received, she could answer their questions. And if they began to show a lack of motivation for their work, as humans often do, Elizabeth would be there to encourage them and help them complete their task.

As the CSR employees performed better, the company grew in ambition. CSR began constructing larger housing complexes, but to do this while maintaining their reputation for efficiency, workers had to erect all the separate modules of the complex at once. More AI Coordinators were needed for this. And so along came someone to oversee the AI foreman in the module next to Elizabeth's, a man by the name of Irwin.

He was of German descent, one of the few grown men Elizabeth knew with golden blonde hair, albeit diluted with several streaks of white. His royal blue eyes sat within a pair of wrinkled orbits, and when conversing with Irwin his eyes seemed to stare through you rather than feign any compassion or even the slightest interest in your words. But Elizabeth had gotten used to this after years of working with him, and she had even come to regard Irwin as a friend. At the very least, she valued his input on the occasional work-related problem. She had always said Irwin had engineering in his blood, not only because his AI foreman and robotic workers ran more smoothly than hers, but because Irwin regarded everything as a logistical problem to be solved, even his human employees.

When it came to managing the complaints of his human staff, Irwin never quite mastered Elizabeth's rapport with the laborers. Elizabeth was good with people because she could understand and empathize with them. She found that a smile and a pat on the back could motivate employees to finish the task far more effectively than Irwin's method: scolding and some occasional threats. To Irwin, the fact that humans couldn't be programmed for peak performance as easily as robots was a nuisance that frustrated him daily.

Elizabeth walked up to the makeshift recreation area, an outdoor lounge of sorts with a few folding chairs, a table with a TV on it and a refrigerator stocked with all types of beverages and a few packed lunches. As she approached, she greeted Irwin who was getting himself a bottle of water from the fridge. "Good morning, Elizabeth," he said. "How was the launch?"

"Oh it was fantastic. You should have seen it up close."

"I am perfectly fine watching it online in the comfort of my bed, thank you," said Irwin as he took a sip. They went on to share their weekend stories with each other. He relayed his accomplishments of the shows he had finished binge watching, and he was happy to have just relaxed and done nothing of vital significance. "That is without a doubt a clear sign I'm getting old," he said.

They soon paused their conversation as a news anchorwoman began reporting the events over the weekend, including the launch.

Whereas the last rocket was headed for Mars to set up another colony there, the news anchor said, *this rocket, launched on Saturday, is expected to reach Titan, one of the moons of Jupiter.*

Irwin shook his head slowly with a hint of disbelief.

"Remarkable," he said. "We are witnessing the epitome of technological achievement. I never thought I'd see interplanetary colonization in my lifetime. Now it's the norm, and I can barely keep up with the latest conquest."

Elizabeth nodded in silence as they gazed at the screen for another brief moment. Then Irwin gulped the rest of his water before they both turned and walked toward their workstations. "Alright, time to make a living," she said. "Meet up for lunch?"

"Of course."

"I'm thinking Thai-Mexican fusion," said Elizabeth grinning sarcastically. With a raised eyebrow he glanced in her direction. She knew Irwin well enough to realize he would never step foot in such a place. "Unless you'd prefer porridge? Gruel, perhaps?"

"Funny," he said, "How about the cultured meat place?"

"Oh yes, they have that sriracha burger I like. You calling the drone or should I?"

Irwin volunteered to contact the delivery service. The pair parted ways and moved to their respective workspaces, two modules separated by fields of green surrounding large patches of upturned mud and rust-colored clay.

As she made her way to her station, Elizabeth allowed herself some reminiscence. Working with the latest version of building information modeling had its thrills, providing her an avenue to explore new housing designs and then bring them to life with the help of her construction crew, but it did present what seemed like thousands of quality issues to deal with every day. At times she longed for the old days of her training with neural networks, when she could design, build and tweak them until perfection. In her past life of strictly coding AI the only issues to troubleshoot were things like assertion error, more her fault than the machine's. At first coding was like learning a foreign language, the struggle to memorize the one-syllable terms before expanding into larger vocabulary. The instant she caught on, coding became a set of Legos, which she could manipulate and combine into more and more complex repetitions. As her proficiency sharpened to a pin the experience of programming transformed until now she was a master chef, unsatisfied with her creation until she herself sprinkled the last garnish of parsley onto her masterpiece. But like anyone with newly bestowed power, especially the power to control and manipulate, it was only right she learned how to wield it in a conscientious way. She made her programming an engine of change, not a loaded weapon.

11

Long before the last evening light over the patrol base would vanish, young, rugged men with short hair and minimal body fat readied their gear and formed a line of muscle covered in rucksacks, helmets, and armored jump-suits. Their suits were a weave of nanofibers, robotic threads so small and woven so tightly that they could not only stop a bullet, but if a bullet hit the jumpsuit, the nanotech in the fibers would push outward in one unified motion, nearly canceling the force of the incoming projectile. Still, most veterans agreed getting shot while wearing this "chain mail" was like whacking your thumb while hammering a nail or being hit with a paintball point blank. The suits had a texture more like plastic than cloth, but sweat still seeped through and the salty residue still caked the fibers after a long day of battle drills.

Their commander, huddled in the center of the patrol base, issued instructions to the leadership team. "UAV picked up a small bunker 16 miles from here." His voice was hoarse from years of vocal cord strain. "We visualize this as a very useful asset to us, so y'all are being tasked to clear this bunker with minimal structural damage."

Among these leaders was Xavier Bojovnik, whose squad was given the task. He was older than the average enlisted man. To an 18-year-old, in fact, he seemed so aged that he earned the fond nickname of Grandma despite being in his late 20s. Still he could run faster, carry heavier equipment, and had a more dedicated work ethic than thousands of his so-called grandchildren. Aside from his towering, brawny stature, Bojovnik's university education allowed him a mature, comprehensive worldview that he maintained even when digging through the mud with his comrades. His etiquette could be as blue collar or erudite as the occasion demanded. He had the respect of his comrades, and when faced with a challenging task he could organize the manpower required. Xavier was a natural leader, and today of all days he would need to be.

"You won't have mortar support or other heavy assets," the commander continued, "but no enemy personnel have been detected. Gain control of the bunker so we can use it for future missions." He nodded. "Get it done."

The troops emptied out of the patrol base like sand through an hourglass, emerging into a field laid bare in the sun. Despite its brilliance, the sun gave little warmth to the grass on this day nor any day in months. Yet still colder was the forest ahead.

The soldiers bid a silent farewell to the sun as they immersed themselves among the dimly lit trees. Facing damp and frigid air, the soldiers marched forth. Step after step, through marshlands that chilled to the bone, they stamped their boot prints in formation. No stopping to nurse an ankle sprain or take pressure off a sore knee. One grueling mile to the next they trudged.

Despite the platoon's perilous journey, an assortment of angels guided them through dangerous territory, shielding them from detection. The treetops helped to mask them from video surveillance. An operator at headquarters sat hunched over a computer console, and from this throne he sent a signal via antenna that interfered with the enemy satellite. In the forest, trotting alongside the troops were robotic dogs. They were waist high, their traditional factory-made gray casing replaced by a camouflage shell with openings for vision and mapping sensors. Their canine legs were slender, their paws rounded stubs capable of gripping any ground surface with ease. Each of these bots wielded a small infrared disruptor with enough range to hide fifty humans.

As the soldiers drew nearer to their target, one reached into his rucksack and removed an electronic pad. He illuminated the screen. Another soldier tossed a UAV forward into the air, and when the drone was high enough it began streaming video and infrared onto the pad.

On video, from the drone's elevation of 500 feet the forest looked like a bed of moss, and the gimbal camera of the drone detected no troop movements amid the trees.

Wind howled upon the men. The sting on Xavier's nose and cheeks was but a distraction from the sensation of ice filling his bones. He focused on his brethren and the trial they faced, and he and his platoon pressed on in a steady cadence with all the efficiency of Caesar's tenth legion.

At last the treeline was in visual range, but before they

reached the edge of the woods, they were faced with a painful truth. They had not moved fast enough.

Rattling machine gun fire sounded in the distance as bullets collided with a number of Xavier's friends. Their muscles stiffened under the hammering, metal turning to plumes of shrapnel around their jumpsuits. Two soldiers were less fortunate, and they collapsed under the barrage, their faces now unrecognizable. All other soldiers dove for cover, returned fire and braced themselves for a fight. The bone chilling cold was now forgotten as projectiles scraped off nearby trees and whizzed by the men before thudding the ground. Amid the splash of mud and splintering of tree bark, Sergeant Bojovnik's men, engaging with their rivals, awaited orders.

The snap of enemy rifles reverberated in the thick foliage. A soldier next to Bojovnik spotted a rustling in a far-off shrub, aimed and fired. His bullet whizzed past the combatant, but this gave his weapon a chance to auto target. With one more squeeze of the trigger he scored a direct hit through his opponent's skull.

Xavier positioned himself behind a large pine tree. His eardrum vibrated as a bullet thumped into the trunk of the tree. Now he knew where the bullet came from, and so did his autotargeter. He emerged just enough to aim and fire a round into the shooter's chest, and the man collapsed to the earth. Bojovnik regained his cover.

The opposition breaking the silence with gunfire meant their bunker was close. Xavier's team had overcome impossible terrain to find it. Taking it would prove a greater challenge. The opponents were renowned for their aggression on the battlefield, despite their limited equipment.

He considered options for his men. "Gimme the readout from the UAV," Sergeant Bojovnik commanded.

The drone relayed clear overhead video footage of what lay in store for the troops. Beyond the wooded marsh, in a clearing sat a large concrete structure. Its outer walls were pristine, free from moss or vines. One wall was interrupted by a solitary black steel door. Aside from the rolling pasture and sporadic weeds, the bunker was clear of any obstructing vegetation for at least 100 yards in each direction. There were a number of openings in the bunker, through which lethal machine gun fire had ended many lives over the stronghold's bloody history.

Now the bunker was within reach for Xavier's band of warriors. He fixed the butt of his weapon against his shoulder. He rolled his back off the tree and rallied his soldiers to continue their advance toward the structure.

They sprang through the brush. As they bounded from tree to tree their rifles burst at the oncoming soldiers. One enemy bullet zipped by Xavier's ear. Another slammed into the ground, splashing mud onto his boot.

He ran to his next cover, followed close behind by a young private named Thompson whose bulging eyes stung with sweat and whose wiry legs jostled with every step of his boots. Xavier crouched behind a mound of shrubs near an old, leafless tree, its bark blanketed with moss. Bullets whirred over his head while he stayed hidden and unscathed.

Private Thompson did not prove fast enough to join him. The young soldier's head jolted backward. His helmet and weapon stamped the earth.

"Thompson's down," said Xavier, dejected at the spectacle.

His sadness gave way to aggression, and he retaliated with several of his own rounds, dropping a foe who had ventured too far from his tree. "Ammo is low," he said on the intercom. No sooner did he end his message than a sound of mechanical gyrating started in the distant trees. It grew louder. With a geared gallop a robotic dog appeared, laced with ammo and supplies around its torso. It dashed at blinding speed, stirring leaves in its wake, until it reached Xavier. On arrival it crouched on all fours. As it scanned the area for advancing forces, Xavier pulled a magazine off its back, latched it into his weapon and commanded the bot to resupply his men.

Gunshots popped in the distance, ripping through the woodland, missing Xavier by inches. He and his team answered. The stocks of machine guns jolted against their shoulders as smoke drifted from their weapons. Within their scopes one adversary after another collapsed out of view, but it was not enough.

More attackers approached, their rifles sending blasts of metal into a number of Xavier's men. His troops needed to clear the woods of any threat before moving on to the bunker so they would not be attacked from behind. They were pinned down, but Xavier had a solution.

"That UAV has a grasp function," he verified over the comm with the drone operator.

"It does."

"Here's what we're gonna do." Xavier instructed the operator where to send the aerial vehicle. He radioed another group with instructions on what to do when they received the drone.

Two more shots collided with Xavier's tree cover as a gang

of fighters trickled toward him. He crouched lower, aimed and pulled his trigger. Another foe in camouflage grunted and dropped into the mud, but the clan kept advancing.

The UAV flew over Xavier to its destination. It descended fast and landed next to one of his nearby friends who reached into his kit and pulled out a pair of small metallic cubes. He tapped each one several times then attached both to the bottom of the drone. "Good to go," he told the remote pilot. The UAV lifted off and darted above the woods. The munitions team, sheltered in the foliage, waited.

On the pilot's pad, video footage skirted over treetops until a red beacon appeared like a bullseye beside one particular tree. "Drop number one," the drone operator radioed to the munitions leader. From above the gang of foes a small cube clinked its way down through leaves and branches until it plopped in the mud beside an enemy boot.

"Detonate."

The press of a button. A blinding flash in the distance followed by a roar louder than thunder. Trees crumbled as brown sludge and stones filled the air.

When the drone approached its second target overtop another group of assailants it released its grip on the other cube. The hostiles could not scatter before, "Detonate!" Another flash and deafening boom unearthed the mud and rocks beneath their feet and incinerated the cluster of enemies. This gave Xavier and his men the chance they needed to regroup.

Puffs of sawdust exploded from tree bark as rival bullets smothered the landscape. Amid the chaos the troops aligned in a formation resembling a crescent moon. Dense greenery filled the space between each soldier, but when the order was issued, they moved as one. A hundred feet ahead lay the forest edge. A setting sun twinkled through the leaves and graced the grassland. To reach it the wedge of troops pushed forward like a spearhead through thick leather. They dashed forth from tree to tree, taking aim when exposed and peppering any visible opponents. One aggressor spun around as his shoulder caved under the impact. Another received a piercing through his throat, lifting him off his feet. Before long the burst of enemy weapons dwindled to the sound of popcorn nearing its completion, and Bojovnik, with his comrades, reached the clearing.

Silence muffled the air. Browning-tinged grass fluttered in the frigid wind. "All clear," a voice over the channel reported to the troops. Welts in their arms, chests and legs reddened and throbbed under the nanofiber suits. Aching and fatigued, the men readied themselves to complete their mission. Despite the assurance of ease they received from the base's mission plan, the men were eager to finish the job and take the bunker.

Xavier led his companions along the border of the forest in a bold flanking maneuver. They crept with soft, efficient steps. Only when they aligned with one side of the bunker did they halt. There stood the gray cubic structure, alone, quiet, rising above the surrounding grass as if it were a tumor disrupting smooth skin. The lawn on one side of the bunker was scarred with several trenches excavated earlier by enormous digger bots in the standard, Z-shaped pattern.

Rifle stalks pressed to shoulders, the troops leveled their weapons at a lonely door centered in the cracking concrete facade of the cube. The SAW gunner crouched down, gluing his belly and legs to the earth. He unfolded the bipod stand for his machine gun and took aim at the door. No one, not drone nor human, saw the secret exit on the other side of the bunker.

A large rectangle of grass lifted from the ground and retracted. Waiting underneath was a host of fresh, battle ready challengers. They crept out one by one with weapons at the ready, and they clustered behind the far wall.

Half the squad, dubbed alpha team, ordered by Bojovnik, left the beta team behind as they exited the cover of trees into the immense clearing. Alpha moved in brisk pace toward the trenches. Still no opponent was in sight. They advanced farther, past the only cover the prairie provided. Friction rubbing from the suits and the soft crinkle of boots stomping over grass were the only sounds. And then, "Down! Down!"

Cracking rifle fire erupted from the far corner of the bunker. Adversaries poured forth, spewing bullets into Alpha team.

From the woods Bravo's SAW gunner squeezed his finger tight. His machine gun jackhammered, streaming deadly projectiles to the enemy. Some hostiles dropped or jolted backward, but others advanced toward the trench.

A loud, rapid metallic clamoring came from the bunker, like a fist pounding on a screen door. As the noise overpowered the clatter in the battlefield, high power rounds cut through the nanofiber suit, flesh, and bone.

"Into the trenches," yelled an Alpha team member. They ran back to the furrows, and in they leapt. One tumbled into the ditch, splashing mud as clumsily as a baby in bathwater, his hamstrings cramping around a raging leg wound. Not all his brothers had made it to the trench in time. Some lay prostrate in the field, their weapons and limbs askew, motionless. Pointed metal whizzed overhead or bludgeoned the ground, sending crumbs of dirt sprinkling over the helmets of the entrenched Alpha team.

In the forest, Xavier's eyes flickered to his visual display. Only nine friendlies still registered beating hearts. They appeared as blue dots sprinkled on the battlefield map. Backup would not arrive for some time. "Let's move out. Follow me," Xavier yelled. Bravo team dashed through the forest edge in single file. Twigs cracked under their boots as they tramped closer to the sound of friendly fire.

Alpha team's rifles flashed above their trench, bursts of blazing metal spewing forth, cutting into the opposing onslaught in a desperate attempt to hold them at bay. One foe dropped into the grass, leaving a lifeless mound of tissue under a drooping helmet. Another was flung backward as a round crashed through his chest. He lay in fetal position, ear pressed to the ground, eyes locked open, blades of grass imprinting his cheek. Yet many more rivals flowed from the bunker, firing with wild belligerence into a darkening horizon.

Bojovnik and the Bravo team were near. They could now engage the enemy in the field, but doing so would announce their presence to the machine gunner in the bunker window. With Alpha under heavy fire, there was little choice.

"Light 'em up," Xavier said. From the cover of trees and mounded earth the riflemen and SAW gunner aimed and squeezed. Their heavy metal weapons sparked to life and kicked against their shoulders. Bullets glimmered in the air, piercing their opponents, knocking them down like spare bowling pins. The surviving foes reached the trench and dove in, and there they stood with weapons pointed at the rest of Alpha team.

A fierce skirmish ensued. Lethal rounds flowed in both directions down the crevasse. Dirt spat onto the soldiers as metal flitted past their helmets and chiseled the excavated walls. As the adversary pressed closer, Alpha's auto targeting advantage eroded until it was gone.

In tight quarters the enemy was all the more fierce. Like berserkers in days of old they growled and wailed as they charged at Alpha team. Up close they bore their gnarled teeth through thick, raggedy beards. Their faces contorted with rage fueled by years of propaganda and imagined slights, overlain with scars from the resulting conflicts. Two Alpha team members took aim and gored the berserker running in front. Without a pause his friends leapt over him and punished the Alphas with a bludgeoning to their heads.

While his comrades continued their vicious assault on Alpha team in the depths of the trench, the shooter in the window turned his heavy machine gun toward the trees. His assistant loaded a weighty belt of pointed metal shells into the chamber. The shooter closed the cover with a snap and a click, pressed himself against the shoulder stock, and centered the crosshairs over Bojovnik.

The barrel of the heavy machine gun let off a metallic clink. This was an unexpected sound. The gunner's eyes widened at the sight of a small cube magnetized to the side of his weapon, and the last he heard was a drone swooping past his window. Then a flash.

Fire, smoke and chunks of cement erupted out of the window with volcanic might. Shrapnel rained upon the soldiers below, but they ignored the rattling on their helmets and kept their rifles blazing, peppering the forest edge.

The tree protecting Xavier thumped and splintered. He allowed himself a brief satisfaction that the drone strike was a success. Then his training took hold. He sharpened his focus. His eyes narrowed, and with expert aim he and his troops rattled a final volley across the field. Hot metal soared at the opposition. A sternum smashed, vital arteries ripped through, lungs punctured. Soon every last enemy not in the trench was lying dead on the grass.

Xavier's team sprang from the forest and ran toward the trenches. He signaled to the trenches that Bravo was on its way, but the response in his earpiece was such a cluster of screams and clashing of metal that his ear ached from the torment. Then the wailing stopped.

Bravo soldiers arrived at one end of the z-shaped excavation. With caution they descended until the dirt walls towered over them. They continued through the muddy trail, breathing heavily yet moving in silence, making not a stone grind under their feet.

They turned the first corner. A pair of adversaries were caught off guard, and they turned too late to face Xavier and his men who drilled bullets into their chest and cranium.

The remaining hostiles in the ditch trudged their boots around the far corner. Their eyes seemed to glare directly into Bojovnik's. Soldiers covered in sweat and spattered blood sprinted at him, but his comrades were ready. With their weapons leveled, they unleashed a hurricane of metal raindrops into the onslaught. Bravo's SAW gunner stepped forward, muddy gravel crushing beneath him. He tightened his grip on his machine gun, found his assailant coming at him in the sight, and juddered a raging torrent of armor piercing alloy at his foe. Bodies stiffened and tumbled forward onto dead comrades. Others flailed backward onto the ground. The attack ceased. Weapons cooled. The berserkers all lay still.

The last smoke wafted to the top of the trench walls where a frosty breeze whisked it across the plains. Fumes danced along and blended with the air, disappearing as they reached the bunker where, one last time, the secret hatch opened. A final crowd of enemy troops emerged. They fanned out with rifles lifted, each man with his head cocked and looking down the sight, surveying the land. Their eyelids squinted from the gleam of evening sun gloriously blinding their retinas. They had not seen the Bravo weapons aimed at them from the edge of the trench. Bojovnik seized this opportunity. He issued the order to fire.

* * *

Sitting at the large wooden desk in front of his classroom, the sergeant faced a sea of teenagers. They were silent, each one staring into a digital pad on a small wooden table suspended above a curved, plastic seat. For a brief moment Xavier allowed his thoughts to drift to his day of honor and bravery, the day the bunker was secured, the mission accomplished. That day he earned his medal. That day the battle was his.

But he was not one for reverie, and a student's question

snapped him back to the present. He hunched over his pad, read the question, and typed a response.

One student slid her headphones off and massaged her ears, her hair crinkled from nearly an hour under direct pressure from the padding.

At another desk, a girl whispered a question into her microphone, the modern way to raise your hand. The speech to text appeared in front of Xavier. He typed, "What is the course and module number?"

"Ancient Civilizations. Babylonian. Question #4."

Xavier accessed the teacher's module resource. His feedback appeared in large print on the white board behind him.

Another question streamed to his pad from an orange haired, gangly youth. A microphone stemmed from the boy's soundproof headset, and he pulled it to his lips. "AI says China's citizens have been under control of the state for generations. But this control helped China rise to superpower status in a very short time. So don't the ends justify the means here?"

Xavier had encountered many such questions born of ignorance. AI gave the students information, but it could not replace a pedagogue's desire that his pupils think outside the box.

Ends do not justify means, but an AI history module does not care if students know this. Xavier, on the other hand, fought hard to impart his class with logic and problem-solving skills. He saw the erosion of critical thinking by reliance on AI as an insidious danger, and he planned to continue fighting this new enemy with the same vigor that had earned him his medal.

12

In a bedroom with dim lighting, a woman lay weak and haggard, her faint cough dusting the white linen of her pillow and sheets. Her unkempt blonde hair frazzled over the beads of sweat on her forehead. The mattress rustled as she rolled over. A damp residue of sweat stained the bedding where her back had lain. Her eyelids seemed to lack the strength for opening, and so she only had a vague awareness of the figure standing over her bedside.

A washcloth gently pressed against her forehead, then over the hair matted on the back of her head. The pain in her muscles set ablaze with the slightest movement, and her bones smoldered when she was still. Medication muffled the pain but also dulled her wits. She didn't say much. She ate even less. She was aware of little else going on in the world aside from her own discomfort. Even her husband leaving for work that morning had escaped her memory.

Another searing jolt electrocuted her as she coughed hard. "It hurts," she groaned with the crackle of an unused voice. The figure by her bed announced something to her she couldn't make out yet understood all the same, and the lightning coursing through her dulled to a tingle.

A few months prior the doctors had come to a consensus. Her illness was terminal. By the time the physicians informed her and her husband there was nothing else they could do, her body had already begun to whither, and the pain had started its roar in her belly and extremities. After repeated attempts at therapy it became clear the most practical approach was comfort care alone.

Her husband had been the strongest advocate for her treatment. He never lost hope, and he always pushed for the most comprehensive care modern medicine could provide. His optimistic outlook was tempered only by her pragmatism. She had always seen the world for what it is and how it works and, as a result, could predict the inevitable outcome.

In preparation she had composed her living will. In it she clearly stated, against her husband's plea, that she wanted to be a DNR. She was not to be resuscitated in the event her heart stopped beating. Performing a full code, on the other hand, was likely to break her ribs from the forceful chest compressions, and if she survived the electroshock from the AED, she would likely have a tube stuffed down her throat before being attached to a ventilator. She had never relished the notion of being dependent on a machine to breathe, perhaps indefinitely. Her husband, on the contrary, had been willing to use any technology available to prolong the life of his bride, giving less regard to what quality of life she may face. Instead, with what little voice she still possessed, she had decided to let nature take its course. She signed and notarized the document, and her wish became bound by law.

Her final step in the process was to register with the hospice service. Here the highest priority was her comfort, preserving her dignity to die in the way she wanted rather than in a hospital riddled with needles and tubes. Hospice arranged a home caregiver to be available at all times and provide medicine to soothe the pain and help her relax.

Devastated though he was, her husband insisted on staying by her side, working with the caregiver, attending to her every need. With soft strokes of his gentle fingers he glided through her hair, clearing the strands from her eyes, placing them behind her ear in continual massage. He whispered to her anything that seemed fitting. The latest updates from her relatives, the news, ancient words from old poets, the latest trends and technology. Their memories together.

As days turned to weeks, somehow within her definite fate a candle of unexpected hope began to glimmer. Her pain seemed more tolerable. With this relief, or with a renewed will, she was able to make it out of her crumpled sheets and, with assistance, squeak into the nearby fluffed leather chair.

More weeks came and went. The sun was becoming obscured by clouds of gray and longer nights as the land cooled, but her illness had not claimed her, much to everyone's surprise. While the husband still offered to wait on her every need she reminded him that, though she appreciated his concern, he needed to be out enjoying his own life rather than worrying about hers.

More time passed. Cool rains blew in, often sideways from the gusting breeze characteristic of the change in season, yet the struggling patient appeared stable. The more she proved she could get by with minor assistance from her caregiver, the more her husband agreed to leave her side. She convinced him to return to work. Now she was all but alone at home, sharing her degenerative experience with only her caregiver during the daytime until her husband returned.

On occasion her symptoms would flare, whether from stress or a virus or overexertion, and the sweating would return as the nerves in her arms and legs sizzled once more. Her caregiver was always there, dialing up the medication as needed, the cool blanket of relief gently coating her inflamed body.

She directed a short, inaudible groan to the side of the bed, and this prompted the caregiver to perform a quick check on her. Near the bed a digital display twinkled with multicolored squiggly lines and corresponding numbers. Heart rate on the lower side but still in normal range. Same with blood pressure and oxygen level. Then, in a breakthrough of cognition, she spoke. "Where is Sebastian?"

The caregiver responded, "Your husband left for work today."

"Do you know when he'll be back," her voice cracked.

"He said he had some errands to run after work, but I'm sure he'll be back this evening. How are you feeling, Yvonne?" Without a response Yvonne shifted her weight all the way to the edge of her bed. She planted both hands on her knees and flexed what little muscle she had. Her legs shuddered as she forced herself to a stand, then an inch at a time she shuffled her feet across the room. The caregiver kept track of her as she moved into the hallway and out of sight. Within seconds the caregiver detected Yvonne's heart rate skyrocket, then the telemetry reading exploded into an angry jagged line of teeth just before the crash sounded in the adjacent room.

The caregiver rushed into the kitchen and found Yvonne sprawled on the tiled floor. Silverware and the shattered fragments of a plate surrounded her. She was motionless, her eyes closed as if resting after a day long and strenuous.

At first the caregiver touched Yvonne's neck and wrist, but there was no pulse. A once vibrant telemetry reading was now a flat line, and the rest of her vital signs were not compatible with life.

The caregiver called Sebastian at work, and in a soothing, preprogrammed voice let him know his wife had passed. The robotic caregiver then lifted the patient with great care and placed her lifeless body on the bed.

Before long Sebastian burst through the door, dropped his coat on the ground and marched toward the bedroom. He saw the caregiver on the way and without stopping asked, "How did this happen? You were supposed to be watching her, weren't you?!" The robot said very little save for a concise relaying of events without excuses. Sebastian's march halted in the doorway of their room. She wasn't moving, not in pain, not in her usual happiness at his arrival. Despite his apprehension, he had to check on her. He had to know if she was really gone. His feet carried him to her bedside. Sebastian called her name. Nothing. He nudged her shoulder, but there was no response from his bride. He pressed his fingers to her, but there was no vibration in her arteries.

Sebastian grasped her hand with his usual gentle hold, but her warmth that used to kindle in his palms now was a leather glove stuffed with bone. A swell of agony filled him.

Tears burst forth as he doubled over, every moment of his lament being observed and recorded by the caregiver. "She was doing better. 'Comfortable, and vital signs stable,' that's what you've been telling me." This time the electronic caregiver made no response.

Yvonne's husband stood up over her bed, clutching her hand in his as tears drizzled down and dripped off his chin. This wasn't how it was supposed to happen. His wife had been in fine spirits. She was comfortable. She seemed happy. He even thought some days maybe she could beat this thing that had been plaguing her body. But now he would never see her smile again, never hear her pleasing words or enjoy her cheek pressed against his when they embraced. It was over.

"Why didn't you do something to help her," he snapped at the caregiver. "You should've called the hospital."

"I'm afraid it was too late for that," said the caregiver.

His chest felt like a vice was closing on it. He snorted up the salty liquid in his nose but it kept leaking onto his upper lip, and he tried not to choke on it as he shouted, "Well then you could have given her CPR. You should've at least tried something. You could've saved her!"

"It was her explicit wish that nothing be done to revive her. She wanted to be DNR, and we must respect that. I know you're hurting, Sebastian, but there was really nothing more we could've done." He glared at the machine, a small flame of hatred now lit and growing steadily within him. Now he saw what was under the bot's hard plastic outer shell, and to Sebastian it was as cold and heartless as any piece of useless machinery in their home. He was now certain this thing in front of him knew nothing about love or respect, not for his wife, not for anyone. And Sebastian would never forget it. Without another word, the doctor turned to look upon the face of his beloved.

* * *

Sebastian reclined on the sofa in his high-rise, one bedroom apartment while reviewing an article from the latest medical journal. The large glass wall in front of him offered a breathtaking view of the city, the light from each household, storefront and streetlamp forming a star-studded landscape. Tonight, on another anniversary of his wife's death, he paused his reading. He focused his gaze on one particular light in the glistening topography. A single lamp shone from the home where he and his love had once lived. It was there Sebastian had learned how fleeting human life can be. Since that time a singular mantra echoed in his head, even louder on this day: *without the ability to feel emotion, one cannot have true compassion.*

13

In The Agora, antique wooden chairs creaked as they up-held patrons leaning toward each other in close conversation. A white glow from the morning sun shone through the immense glass wall facing a bustling street. The silhouettes cast within gulped their beverages, held hands, munched, and conversed. As the light spread around the contented figures, it landed on the empty seat reserved for Elizabeth. A scented stimulant sat on the table, placed there by her friends, and it gently propelled steam up to the dark tiled ceiling, the intricate designs of which revived the art deco halls of a past industrial age. Sebastian and Xavier reclined with their ceramic mugs in hand.

"So I'm thinking of investing more in those nuclear fusion companies you love so much," Xavier said.

Sebastian nodded. "It's the future, my man. And it's way better than those soda companies you're invested in now."

Xavier shrugged. "I put my money in products the average person wants, and it pays off."

"Come to the light side." Sebastian winked. "Clean,

renewable energy *is* what the average person wants, even if they don't know it."

"Trouble is," Xavier continued, "the market's been looking like a seismograph last month. The AI algorithms have been a little heavy handed with their high-frequency trading."

"Well, that's what brokers get," Sebastian said, speaking in gestures as much as words. "They tell an algorithm to automatically trade when stocks hit a certain number. Then they dust off their hands and walk away, only to turn back and say, 'Uh oh, what's the machine doing?' But too late, the AI's already done a million trades in a few nanoseconds."

Xavier brushed aside the cautionary tale with a wave of his hand. "Been years since algorithmic trading caused any major market downturns."

"Yeah, but we still don't know why it caused the crashes."

Xavier shrugged. "In those days AI was a black box."

"Sometimes it still is."

The glass facade of The Agora reflected the current customers as ghosts layered over a backdrop of azure blue outside. Etched within the transparent wall was the entry door, and Elizabeth pushed it open, causing the entire panorama of coffeehouse reflections to distort and zoom across the door in an instant. As she shuffled into her seat, Xavier recruited her expertise. "Are we any closer to understanding why AI does what it does?"

"For sure," she nodded. "Our tracking of AI's decision process is way better now. It has to be. You don't want a rogue AI deciding anything unless you know exactly how it arrived at its conclusion. Transparency is one of the foundations of good AI."

"And how do you make sure its decisions are transparent," the doctor asked, not yet a believer.

She shrugged one shoulder, revealing the answer was simple, at least to her. "We stay in the loop, making sure the AI does nothing important without our approval. This means constantly testing the machines. From day one of production we're running different inputs to see what outputs the AI gives us. Alert systems flag us if anything unexpected occurs. Any abnormality and we pause, inspect, and correct it." She drew in the scent of charred chocolate melded in tropical fruit, the latest from Papua New Guinea. She imbibed just a little, trying to absorb each sip with all her senses.

"Nice to hear," Sebastian said, "but even AI built precisely to specifications can still be biased in its decisions. What's to stop a bank's AI algorithm from denying a loan to someone because of their race or gender, or even their age, religion or marital status, just because it's programmed to?"

"The Fair Credit Reporting Act of 1970," said the history teacher. "The Equal Credit Opportunity Act of 1974."

"Okay," Sebastian said, lifting a hand to halt his friend before a full lecture ensued. "So algorithms can't use our protected data. How do we know AI won't use all the other unprotected data to make a biased decision, maybe combining data points we couldn't anticipate?"

"Like what?" Elizabeth was patient, her question probing and without condescension.

"What if the algorithm finds that people from this postal code," he pressed his finger on the table, "who changed jobs more than five times," his finger zigzagging along the wood, "are less likely to repay the bank? Should they be denied a loan?"

Elizabeth savored the hint of pineapple within her heated mug before clearing her throat. "You hope to avoid that kind of bias in AI by gathering good quality data. You need to train AI on large populations that really represent us. Avoid data from small samples, or your AI might come to the wrong conclusion."

"Or worse," Sebastian said, "small sample data could reinforce bias."

Xavier said, "Remember there's a lot of history in data. A data set isn't just numbers, it's a reflection of the culture. It's not as objective as people think."

"And it needs to be scrutinized," Sebastian said, having done his share of analytics in the research field.

Elizabeth offered a solution that, to her, seemed an obvious part of the engineering process. "If you're a bank, credit bureau or mortgage lender, and you want to avoid bias in your algorithm, you simply validate the algorithm. Make sure all your data gets collected the same way. Then you should publicly disclose any key factors your AI used to decide someone's risk score."

"Take it a step further," Xavier said. "Every AI should come with a sheet that says which data trained it."

Sebastian gave his support with a nod. Then he posed a question that gnawed at him. "So who's responsible if a customer still gets treated unfairly because of a biased algorithm? The bank? I'm guessing not the AI."

Elizabeth considered such a situation. "Wouldn't the bank,

and the tech firm that supplied the AI to the bank, share in the responsibility?"

"Sounds like a legal mess," Xavier said.

Sebastian released an audible exhale. "Part of me wishes for simpler days when someone could get a loan based on the quality of their character, not a checklist of numbers and metrics." Xavier shot him a quizzical stare that pierced right between his ears. "I'm saying," he continued, "in ancient times, human judgment and a lender's relationship with the borrower guided the decision to lend. That might've been the only hope for poor folk to gain wealth and have a better chance at life."

"Fine speech, George Bailey," Xavier said, "but in those days a lot of bad loans were given, then brutal tactics were used to collect them. At least today financial institutions know it's wrong to lend money to someone who can't repay it."

"Exactly," Elizabeth said, "and if algorithms direct loans only to people who can safely repay the money, thereby protecting the customer, then shouldn't we use them?"

Xavier took another swig and placed the brew of burnt chocolate and citrus on the table. "You talk about relationships, but it's always been about the numbers. Man or machine, you rely on data to make a decision. Even when one man is determining another's character, he's doing a calculation, adding all the factors in his head."

"We do make calculations," the doctor interjected, "but where we differ from machines is the emotional quotient, that gut feeling that tells us, 'this guy's trustworthy' or 'she deserves a chance, let's give her the loan'."

Xavier said, "Small time lenders may have some room for

compassion in their judgment, but in a big business there's little place for emotion, and none in an algorithm."

"So your question is," Elizabeth said, directing her attention to Sebastian, "can human judgment be accurately represented by an algorithm when deciding to give loans or extend credit?"

He nodded. "Can metrics take the place of human intuition, and should they?"

Elizabeth tossed some mental chips into the proverbial pot to up the ante. "Couldn't the same be said of AI in almost any arena? What if an algorithm in the courts is fed data that says people from a certain poor neighborhood, who have certain characteristics, are more likely to commit a crime if released on bail? If you're from that neighborhood, should you be denied bail and be placed back in a holding cell?"

"No," Xavier said.

"No? Not even for the safety of the community?"

He shook his head slowly and with purpose. "You're talking about correlation. We need justice based on consequence, where punishment comes after you commit a crime, not because you're more likely to."

"Unfortunately," Sebastian said, "if a judge is told that an algorithm uses the latest and best software, he may be more accepting of its conclusions. He might be more likely to sentence innocent people just because they happen to fit a certain profile." Sebastian crossed his arms, forging wrinkles in his dress shirt sleeves. "Which, by the way, would compound the problem. Once someone's labeled 'high risk', they'll be watched more closely, then they'll be more likely to get arrested, which feeds into the bias against them. That cycle brings more injustice to an already disadvantaged people."

"Well, algorithms understand math, not justice," Elizabeth said.

Xavier hooked his fingers through his white ceramic handle and drew the liquid close to his lips. "We've already seen a similar situation with predictive policing. Flagged neighborhoods got more surveillance, which detected more crimes, sending more police to that neighborhood, leading to more arrests, making the neighborhood go higher on the watch list." The last word echoed into the mug before he drank.

"But has surveillance and arrests increased as much for white collar crimes," Elizabeth asked, answering her own question with a scoff.

"Trouble is," Sebastian said, "even if facial recognition or crime detection were 100% accurate, its success would only reinforce surveillance."

"And increased surveillance may catch more crimes, but it erodes the trust between police and citizen," Xavier said.

"Especially when a cop detains someone because a machine profiled them as suspicious," Sebastian said. "Only thing worse is when a police bot detains and searches someone. That's an injustice in itself."

"Why," Elizabeth inquired. "What's the difference if a human cop or android cop stops you?"

Sebastian said. "At least if you're a human cop you can connect with the people you're serving and understand them better. It's hard enough for the police to earn people's trust, but at least human cops can feel the pulse of their community and build a network of information sharing with the citizens.

But if the citizens don't trust them it becomes that much harder for police to connect and to help. With robots that trust is already strained. It's almost an 'us versus them' the minute a machine tells you what to do," Sebastian's eyelids narrowed, "and nobody wants an AI deciding your fate."

"Tell it to people in that Way of the Future religion," said Xavier.

"Or people on dating sites who find true love," said Elizabeth.

The doctor pondered for a moment, ingested another gulp of caffeine, and answered. "Look, in my line of work we're constantly inundated with new technology. Researchers produce it, then reps push it on us. But no matter what dazzling tech innovations we use, one thing'll never change: any important, life-altering decisions about a person should be made by humans, not machines."

Three companions enjoyed the scents of fresh grounds from the Papua islands. Pleasing aromas and engaging company made this Elizabeth's favorite time of day, and her years at The Agora were beginning to infuse in her an appreciation for social interaction without technology. Still, technology would occupy her the rest of the day.

When the trio finished their daily meeting, they sipped their last and proceeded to their separate vocations. Though the work hours were never long, the day ahead would take a heavy toll, more than any of the friends could imagine.

14

Elizabeth reclined in a plush seat, its faux leather casing wrinkled from years of pressure and sheering. Around her sat a number of other patrons squeezed into worn pillowed backrests. They stooped their necks over their devices, headphones in one or both ears, as they were all escorted to their places of work.

The patrons were traveling in an automated van. Through hints of fog on its windows, Elizabeth observed acres of farmland flickering past her eyes as the van sped along the highway. Far above a driverless tractor, swarms of drones sibilated as they surveyed the fields. The soil was rich and dark brown. Agribots had fertilized it enough to grace it with long rows of luxuriant green. Any weed tainting the ground had been identified on a drone camera, marked with a red rectangle, and targeted for elimination. When the drones had relayed the target location to a giant white cube perched on black treads, Elizabeth had the fortunate timing to glimpse what happened next.

Up and down the fields the white mammoth rolled, and under its belly white lights flashed as every targeted weed disintegrated in a miniature lightning strike. A solitary pale blue farmhouse rested beside the field. Although the windows were obscured by towering shrubs, Elizabeth could imagine a single farmer inside, feet upon his desk, coffee mug held over his lap, guiding the whole process from a desktop computer.

The van jostled as it made several turns, at last reaching Elizabeth's destination. Her construction site lay still that morning. Half built apartments exposed their bare metal bones. Not a person walked among the piles of paneling or the bundles of rebar, and all the construction bots sat immobile as stone. No sound could be heard except exuberant birds chirping in nearby trees, the leaves of which were silhouetted with gold as the sun touched upon the landscape.

One by one cars, vans and trucks arrived from all directions. Some entered the parking area while others stopped only long enough to let out passengers brandishing scuffed boots and tool belts. Of all the arriving vehicles, only a few held a person behind the wheel.

For financial reasons, Elizabeth had long ago opted for driverless carpool, a popular form of public transportation among those looking to save on fuel cost and automobile maintenance. She emerged and waved goodbye to her ridesharing crew, then she made her way toward the locker room.

Fine particles of dirt puffed up around her as each long stride molded her bootprint into the ground. Entering the locker room to pick up her hard hat she ran across Irwin. "Hello, Elizabeth," he greeted, his face as expressionless as the walls surrounding them. Over the years, she had learned this was his baseline countenance. In fact she grew to appreciate it as the perfect complement to his dry sense of humor. In stark contrast, Elizabeth bore a wholehearted smile as she wished him good morning. "So," said Irwin, "which planet do you think a rocket will pass by today?"

She scoffed, signaling her response would involve some exaggeration. "Probably the Icarus star system."

Irwin stared blankly.

"It's somewhere between the edge of the universe and infinity." She mused for a moment, picturing the spacefarers' impossible journey to reach places civilians like her could only see on a screen.

With his visage wry and unwavering, Irwin said, "Sounds good. Let's go *there* for lunch today."

"Eh, I bet the price to park is outrageous," she said. "There is that new steak restaurant up the road we could try."

Irwin's face scrunched as though he'd eaten a lemon. "Isn't that the place that serves lab grown meat?"

"Yeah, so?"

"Guess I prefer my cow the old-fashioned way," said Irwin.

Elizabeth kept her sarcasm playful. "Smelly? Slaughtered? A massive drain on resources?"

"Natural."

"Y'know what's natural? E. coli. Other harmful microbes. Cultivated meat has none of that. And it can feed tons more people."

His eyelids flickered. This was the way he expressed disbelief in another's doctrine. "I would've thought you'd have chosen one of the dozen restaurants around here with their own vertical farm out back. Get some fruits and veggies. Instead you wanna get cloned meat?"

She paused for effect. "They serve wooly mammoth."

He sighed to profess one last objection. "See you there." Elizabeth fastened her hard hat firmly over her auburn hair and exited the door at one end of the temporary cuboid room. She strode across the site, though bits of plastic and metal strewn about the dirt, circumventing large clusters of tubing to her right or mounds of wall panels and floor tiles to her left.

When she entered her worksite a number of construction employees greeted her. "Morning, guys," she said as she walked through the group of laborers. Each of them wore a similar outfit: a t-shirt, jeans or khakis, tool belt, work boots and a black wristband with a digital information display. She asked how everyone was doing as she moved past the crowd on her way to the control station.

They all answered. Then one of the workers in the group named Vince, a rather stocky man in his 40s with a dark tan wrinkled face from years working in the sun, reported to Ms. Foster, "Boss, we got an alarm on the hydraulics of platform 3. Looks like they're causin' the printer to spit out two millimeters off. Had to shut 'er down."

A woman from the group who went by the name of Kat, also tan from her job but with stringy bleach blond hair and an impeccable set of white teeth, told Elizabeth, "There's also a warning on the nozzle height, so of course we haven't even been able to put down the first layer yet."

"Not again. Does that printer ever plan on cooperating?" Elizabeth asked.

Kat said, "It has more bugs in it than Vince's bed." The stocky man chuckled. Kat handed Elizabeth a digital pad. "Here's the complete list." A rectangular, coal black rim bordered a dimly lit screen displaying today's bullet points. Then Kat walked alongside her boss to the control center. "Windows are in for apartment 2, and furnishings are started on unit 1. Slicer settings are all good for 3. Oh, and we just got that new supply of locally sourced materials."

"More sand and glass?" Elizabeth glanced up from the pad to see Kat nodding.

"This one has hemp," she said.

"Nice. Hempcrete oughta give us all the support material we need. I'll fix the glitches so we can get rolling. Can you make sure the electricians in unit 2 get their wristbands?" Kat gave a quick salute. "Thanks," Elizabeth said, patting the shoulder of the blonde woman. "Let's hit it hard today. And remember, we're not just building apartments," she said, holding two sarcastic thumbs up, "we're building memories." Kat let air escape through her nose to form a muffled laugh. Then she left Ms. Foster to manage three simultaneous construction projects.

Elizabeth entered the control center, a windowless workroom 10 feet wide and 20 feet long. Gray square panels lined the interior walls and ceiling. Soft white lights overhead flickered on one by one in a march down the ceiling. Soon the room turned from an uninviting pitch-black void to a cozy workspace where she could complete her tasks free from outside distraction.

On a large computer monitor Elizabeth tapped in her password. Her signature letters, numbers and symbols formed a dotted line inside the text box. Then the facial recognition prompt appeared on her phone. She straightened her device, then placed it on the desk, her gaze never breaking from the computer. Her fingers leapt onto the keyboard, pattering through a few more screens until an image appeared at the center of the monitor. The apartment complexes lay unfinished outside, now in full view on her live video feed. She pressed the tips of her five fingers onto a black rectangle beside the computer. She splayed her fingers wide and pulled her hand away from the rectangle. The live video of the whole housing complex, with every employee busily working, was now suspended in the middle of Elizabeth's workspace in a brightly colored holographic display.

She raised her hand to eye level, and the hologram of the apartments rose with it. With her spare hand, Elizabeth grasped the water bottle she kept on her desk. She sipped at it while spreading her other palm again and again until the hologram filled the room.

She turned back to the monitor and typed in a few more commands. Several yellow arrowheads appeared in the hologram over the areas of malfunction. "All right, let's see what the trouble is." She flicked her wrists and moved her arms in various directions, zooming into areas of concern on the holographic image and swiping away any figures blocking her view. First, she removed construction materials and machinery. Zeroing in, she sideswiped miniatures of workers on the ground. She removed the large drones buzzing overhead dropping off supplies to bots on the roof. Past the wavelike walls that undulated in and out in elegant fluidity, she zoomed in toward the towering printers extruding their mixture in layers of soft serve. "Where are you, little gremlins?"

The time had come to make use of the AI Foreman voice recognition software. Since Elizabeth had to interact with it on a daily basis, she could not resist giving it a name. For the foreman she chose the name of her favorite conductor from a bygone age. Pressing in her earpiece she enunciated, "Okay, Muti, show me the nozzle for the printer on housing unit three please."

A crescendo of violins and brass of the old Chicago Symphony Orchestra resounded for a second or two in her ear. Then a pleasant voice chimed, "Good morning, Ms. Foster." The AI Foreman vocalized the height of the nozzle to the second decimal place. In the earpiece the foreman whispered the recommended height based on the architectural plans. Elizabeth returned her attention to the monitor. Her hands slid to the left and right, up and down, only pausing for brief moments so her fingers could perform their rapid dance routine over a keyboard. She placed the digital pad Kat gave her onto a charging platform embedded in her desk. "Read the problem bullet points out loud please," she said, her eyes searching the holographic scene.

Elizabeth appreciated the efforts of all the workers on display. Although she played an essential role for CSR Construction, she never assumed to be more than another cog in the wheel. Kat, Vince and the other human laborers all worked tirelessly alongside the robots. Together they would install the prefabricated walls, ceiling, plumbing, electrical, ventilation and insulation. The humans and bots could create a symphony of hammers banging and saws buzzing, drones whirring and boots stomping, and the thud of air compressed nails driven into place. Driveways and walkways would be poured, flooring and countertops installed, and bathroom fixtures fixed, all by both human and robotic workers. What made this possible, the brain of the operation, was the AI Foreman. Under Muti's direction, bots on wheels could place flooring and wall tiles with accuracy to the micron. The human workers would get a buzz on their wrist bands, read the instructions meant only for them, and proceed to their next assigned workstation. Outside, at the foreman's command, an automated tractor would soon be scraping a land leveler over chunks of dirt and rock, making it smooth and ready to be beautified with green. At the end of the day, the AI Foreman would scan the whole building and call the workers inside to clean up the crumpled trash, shavings, dust and torn snack wrappers. Muti could even inform them what is garbage and what is reusable. Never had there been a more efficient building and cleanup process. As a result, nobody questioned the level of control the AI Foreman possessed.

15

The workday was in full swing. Sturdy construction drones buzzed about the site. They wielded the tips of hoses, spraying sealant over the outer walls and roof. Hefty trucks rumbled and beeped in repetition. A harsh melody of grinding and whirring joined in chorus with the constant growl of industrial machinery.

Isolated in her office, with its soundproof walls muffling the outside noise to a low din, Elizabeth steered her fingers through the worksite. She rotated the entire hologram as if sliding her hands around a globe. Just as she spread her arms wide to zoom in, another blinking yellow indicator appeared. This one was not on the list Kat had given her. Like the other flashing beacons, it hovered over a malfunction, but this time it was in an unexpected place.

Her eyelids squinted. "What's this?" No answer from Muti. She typed a few phrases to isolate the problem. According to the computer, however, there was no issue. All was well, read the monitor. Yet the bright beacon still remained, a rotating arrowhead pointing directly at the server for the AI Foreman.

Elizabeth pressed her earpiece in deeper and said, "Muti, diagnose the server error."

"Evaluation complete," answered Muti. "No error found." The holographic projection ran on a separate system than the foreman. It was another way to monitor key functions of the construction project in case one system malfunctioned.

"Check again. See if your infrastructure monitoring is off." The foreman repeated its statement in the same inoffensive tone. Her frustration became a sarcastic thought. *Did you try unplugging it and plugging it back in?*

Elizabeth grabbed her pad and marched out toward the foreman's server, a cluster of circuits and cables covered in a smooth rectangular black prism. Crouching over it she accessed a control panel on its side.

Her fingers leapt onto the panel and bounced with the vigor of an expert pianist, pausing only to move her hand back toward the pad she was holding and stamp a series of buttons.

Some workers approached, lugging tools and cables. She signaled to them with a motion of her head. "What's goin' on, boss," asked the sweaty one on the right.

"You guys getting any weird instructions on your wristbands? Anything out of the ordinary?"

They examined their wearables for a moment, angling themselves to shadow their screens from the sun. "Mine's blank," one said. The other smacked his wristband, hoping it would somehow reboot. "Gettin' nothin' at all," the sweaty one said. Through her earpiece Elizabeth called over Irwin who was familiar with the foreman's quirks.

"Foreman acting up again, Elizabeth," he asked on his approach.

"I'm getting some conflicting readouts. Holo shows yellow over the server, but Muti says nothing's wrong."

Irwin crammed his glasses against his face. "Might be a problem with the detection grid."

"Maybe. But there's something else that doesn't make sense. I ran a diagnostic just now, and it flagged some lines of code that shouldn't be there." She squinted up at him as he hunched over the digital pad. "It's almost like—"

Her words were overtaken by a faint but growing hum. It rose above the cacophony of construction. All the heads in the worksite turned upward and froze in bewilderment.

High above them was a sight none in the company had ever seen. A hundred feet overhead a mass of scattered black dots congealed into a thin line. The line slid through the air like a javelin, hurling toward the onlookers. A single file column of drones came slicing through the sky. The buzz of their propellers grew deafening as the stream of whirling blades descended onto the workers.

Darting toward the group with furious speed the drones broke off one by one until each had its target in sight. The humans scrambled.

One worker dashed toward the door of the lounge. As he ducked low, a drone grazed the back of his helmet. The hard plastic hat crunched against his scalp, but he kept running for the door. When another drone swooped low and slammed the back of his leg, his knee buckled, and he fell hard onto his elbows. A third heavy drone smashed the side of his ribs, knocking the wind out of him. He gasped for breath, but he was paralyzed as drone after drone pummeled his back and ribcage.

Vince ran behind a mound of stones. He reached his sanctuary and bent over, panting from his first sprint in years. He straightened himself and dabbed the sweat off his brow. When his arm fell away, a drone flew into his face, blinding him as it knocked him off his feet.

Another worker ran in zig zags. Her heavy boots made her steps clunky and slow. Then a sting, like a door jamming a finger, shot into the middle of her back. She stumbled. A plume of dust erupted around her as she struck the ground. She rolled over in time for a drone to nosedive into her windpipe.

Elizabeth narrowly escaped a drone swooping in to decapitate her. It sheared the top of her helmet and knocked it clear off her head. She and several other workers raced to shelter. Some hid near piles of building materials, others behind the 3D printing vehicle. Irwin dashed behind a robotic exoskeleton used for manipulating heavy equipment and massive rocks. It was the perfect protection. Its long metallic arms and agile fingers could handle the weight of 1000 lbs. of force. The arms protruded from a chrome thorax resting on triangular treads, and they remained extended around Irwin as if hugging him, unwavering despite the surrounding tumult.

A drone zipped overhead of Irwin. He flinched, but as the drone flew out of sight, he eased into a stand again. Sounds of distant screaming seemed to echo across the construction site. The cries of Irwin's comrades filled his ears. Then the same drone appeared again. This time it hovered over him. A gentle breeze drifted down from the propellers. This drone was clutching something. A hose. Irwin foresaw the danger just in time. He heaved his legs into motion, firing every muscle fiber to evade. He hadn't gotten but a few feet away before a large metal clamp squeezed around his torso, lifting him in the air and pressing in his sides. His breath drained from him, there was no room left in his lungs for more, and as he was rotated slowly backward in midair, he caught sight of the enormous impregnable arm just before it hurled him to the ground. The drone positioned the nozzle an inch from Irwin's mouth. A flood of sealant erupted at his face. He tried to roll away, but all his might failed him, as though he were trapped under a bulldozer. Then the bulldozer pushed back, squeezing him into the muddy sealant surrounding him. His head writhed, but the drone kept in line with his mouth. Liquid sealant blubbed out of every orifice. His vision darkened, but there was no final exhale of mortality. There was no exhale at all.

Kat and Elizabeth sat hunched in the shade behind columns of tile. Elizabeth tapped wildly on her pad. She accessed remote command functions, pressed in her earpiece, and shouted, "Muti, cease all operations!" The drones continued flying in all directions undeterred. She repeated the command to no avail. Turning to Kat she said, "I have to get to the control panel."

"Not alone," she responded, grabbing a hammer and squeezing her grip around it until her knuckles were white. Then sunlight glimmered onto Kathy's face. Her blonde hair glowed brighter and brighter, next her shoulders, chest then abdomen. The tiles were being lifted off one by one as the drones took turns hauling them away. Their protection dwindling to nothing, Kat yelled, "Go!"

They sprang up and started running just as a drone darted past Kat's head. It turned midair and descended once again. This time it met with the crushing blow of Kat's hammer. The drone shattered and barrel rolled into the dirt, followed by debris sprinkling around it like a hailstorm.

Elizabeth reached the server. Sweat trickled into her eyes. She blinked hard and pressed her thumb on the override button to power down the whole system. Nothing. "System's been bypassed somehow," she yelled to her friend. Using her years of muscle memory she danced her fingers over the panel.

Kat reached her side and stood ready. Two more drones came toward them, their propellers whizzing high above the ground but descending fast. Outside her peripheral vision, the twin treads of the exoskeleton carried the menacing mechanical arms toward her. The arms reached out, metal pincers spreading wide to ensnare their target.

On the panel Elizabeth reached the Foreman control settings. She typed in several lines of code causing a series of prompts to appear. As the duo of drones approached Kat, they separated so one targeted her head and the other her leg. Her eyes narrowed, she aimed and swung her hammer, but the machines were too fast, and Kat's head was knocked sideways as her leg lifted out of the dust like a drunken roundhouse kick. Ribs and muscle rammed into hard earth. Kat's head snapped toward the ground. Her neck muscles seared under the strain. Elizabeth worked her hands over the panel.

As Kat lay stunned, the crystal blue sky above her was slowly eclipsed by moving spindle fingers.

Just a few more sequences of code. The spindles grew into long, mechanical arms that reached for Kat. Elizabeth executed the final command.

All drones, every one of them over her three-unit construction site, floated to the ground as if they had their own parachutes, and the exoskeleton froze. Elizabeth caught her breath as she stared in silence at the machine, its arms extended and fingers poised to grab whichever of Kat's limbs was within reach.

Elizabeth sat immobile, propped against the control panel. Her thoughts now inched along like molasses. Despite the carnage that lay before her she saw nothing. Her ears filled with cotton. Her fingers immersed in ice water. The machines, the humans, all frozen in time.

"Boss," Kat creaked through her dried vocal cords, never breaking her gaze from the looming metal above her. "What's going on?"

The cloud of dust that had filled the air drifted down and sprinkled over the bodies on the ground. Some were squirming, one was not.

Elizabeth stood over her friend. She had never seen someone murdered before, yet Irwin lay in the soil, encased in glue, the contorted anguish on his face preserved forever. She turned away as her intestines twisted. Acid filled her stomach. The bitter taste of bile burned as it spewed from her esophagus.

Soon after placing the 911 call, medical drones entered the area. They flew over Elizabeth to land beside a survivor.

Within minutes ambulances arrived with paramedics leaping out to load the injured workers. "Are you alright, miss," they asked Elizabeth. She stared at them without a word. She rubbed the top of her head, a dull ache reminding her of the helmet that saved her life. When she finally nodded yes, they encouraged her to seek medical attention, but she declined. They jumped back in their vehicle and drove off, rear tires grinding their way out of the gravel, leaving a shroud of dust surrounding Elizabeth. As the wheel of her mind creaked and started turning again, she recalled the four pillars of construction all workers had to learn: "Quality, Safety, Schedule, and Cost."

16

A solitary police car rode along the field surrounding the construction site. Particles of dust clung to its pristine undercarriage, coating the newly washed plastic and metal with a film of brown. Inside the car, a couple officers exchanged jokes. Their car slowed to a halt, and the jokes stopped when they took in the scene. Flashing lights of ambulances and squad cars decorated the mounds of dirt and blanketed the scattered mechanical equipment in shades of red and blue. One ambulance rolled through the dust toward a worker in a hard hat squatting over her injured colleague. She was unwrapping a field kit from a nearby medical drone. It issued instructions in a soft, monotone voice.

The radio in the squad car vibrated chatter to the officers. They pushed open their doors, pupils dilating in full alert as they navigated through the tumult. Every move of the officers anticipated danger. They passed by paramedics bandaging an injured worker. He groaned; his reddened shoulder exposed through a tattered sleeve. Another employee clutched her throat, trying to distract from the pain of swallowing through inflamed muscle and cartilage. The officers stopped to make sure she was alright. It was much easier for her to nod without speaking.

They continued on their way, past more medical drones landing, each voicing the same instructions when they touched ground, "Press top button to open." Then they spotted two workers up the hill who appeared able to give testimony. Their clothes were wrinkled and smeared with dirt, but at least these witnesses were upright and able to speak. With digital pads at the ready, the officers approached Kat and Elizabeth.

"May we ask you some questions," asked the elder. With solemn tone they relayed disturbing details to the officers. From their testimony, it seemed plausible that this was a coordinated attack rather than a construction accident, and it was intended to cause maximum harm.

When they had gathered enough information, the police asked if Kat and Elizabeth minded staying on site for a while. "You can find me right here," Elizabeth replied, pointing toward the control panel. The two men closed their screens and strode back to their car. Kat made the call to workplace safety and health. Elizabeth got to work on the consol.

Her attention to the tiny symbols of code on the control screen never wavered, even when Kat placed a comforting hand on her. Elizabeth had lost a friend, but the gentle pressure on her shoulder helped to quell the despair writhing in her. With renewed vigor, she vowed to herself not to rest until she uncovered the reason her friend was killed.

The officers neared their vehicle. The senior officer spoke so only his adjacent partner could hear. "What are your thoughts?"

"Pretty nasty," responded the junior.

"That your professional opinion?"

"Well," the junior glanced back at the bustle of medical drones and paramedics, "I'd say there's no way this was some construction accident."

The senior nodded. "Better call in Homicide."

"I hate these robot crimes. They never leave behind DNA or fingerprints, and they don't follow the usual human motives."

"Let's not jump to conclusions," the senior said, dabbing his forearm against the sweat from his hairline. "Just because it's carried out by robots doesn't make the robots responsible."

"Yeah? How so?"

"These bots aren't like those general AIs that can think and act on their own. Construction bots are all easy to control, and they usually don't make a move without being told to by a human." They scrunched into the front seats, slammed the doors, and sent their message to headquarters.

At the police department, the crime scene investigators on call received a notification. The crackled voice of the control dispatcher, laced with occasional static, briefed them on what to expect. Fast and focused, the CSI officers gathered their supplies, loaded them into their vehicle and departed.

When they arrived, they taped off the scene. The CSI team was meticulous with the evidence, taking such care not to disturb the area that everything inside their yellow tape appeared frozen in time.

Then came the detectives. A woman with prominent cheekbones and a sharp mandible exited one side of an unmarked car. She swiped her coal black hair away from her eyelashes then straightened her sportscoat with a tug. From the other side of the car emerged a dark figure. His sunken eyes matched the rest of his gaunt features. Despite his height, the hunch in his back contorted him into something like an old, hollowed out tree bereft of any green. Together the detectives strode through the open field, which was speckled with large machinery and immobile, innocent-looking drones.

They surveyed the premises, taking detailed notes. They discussed their findings as they tracked down and interviewed all the workers lucky enough to avoid the hospital. After every last witness issued a testimony, most of which conveyed sheer consternation at the atrocity, the detectives approached Elizabeth. They stood above her as she tapped away at a screen. The hollow tree cleared his throat. This did not elicit the desired effect. Eventually they had to call her attention to their badges. She stood and acknowledged them. They asked their questions, and Elizabeth told them what happened. She informed them of her role at CSR Construction, and when they asked about her history as a programmer, she told them that too.

Once they'd finished their open-ended questions, out came the verbal tweezers. One by one they picked out the bits of information they needed.

"In all your years doing this," the woman with chiseled features asked, "ever seen anything like this before?"

"No."

"Ever hear of anything like this before?" This yielded

the same answer. "Any idea what could have made the bots do this?"

An image flashed in her mind. The odd lines of code on the screen. At this time, however, she did not have enough information to form a hypothesis. Her pointed chin glided across her neck. "No."

"In your role here you can enter commands to directly control the bots' actions. Could you have entered in something by mistake?"

"You mean a line of C++ that says 'kill all humans'? No."

The detectives shot a quick glance at each other, unamused. They thanked her and ended her interview by issuing the same advice to her as they had to every other employee. "Don't leave town."

Soon it would be time to examine the evidence. The detectives planned to assess how often the machines and equipment were tested for malfunctions, to check the mechanical specifications on the machines and where they were manufactured, to request access to the video footage from the drones, and to find out how much autonomy each robot had. When dealing with a murder scene, one that leaves so many tearful survivors in the wake, a singular thought permeates every member of the homicide division and instills in them a fire of determination: *justice must be done.*

* * *

At the end of it all an exhausted Elizabeth trod wearily toward her carpool ride. The driverless van made its way toward her home via the standard routes, with only her ride-sharing friends in the back able to detect the changes in her usual jolly expression.

She opened her apartment door to a hardworking Teresa. Her roommate put down the mop as soon as she observed Elizabeth's concerning behavior, the subtle differences that only a friend or a family bot programmed with a high emotional quotient might notice. "Hey. What's up," Teresa asked open-endedly. Elizabeth knew her friend as a true confidant, one that would keep matters private, pass no judgment, and offer insights outside the realm of typical human thought. She relayed the entire day to the unwavering attention of Teresa who offered consolation only when appropriate, and then together they began troubleshooting the possible causes of the catastrophe. Before making much progress, their efforts were interrupted by an incoming call.

"Miss Foster," asked a gruff voice. "We'd like you to come down to detective headquarters, homicide division."

17

A building of red brick studded with gray corner stones towered over Elizabeth. She approached the front entrance, and a pair of sliding glass doors opened as if inviting her. In the lobby the AI concierge greeted Elizabeth and directed her toward Homicide. She walked down the labyrinthine hallway making a series of lefts and rights, all the while silent glowing yellow arrows flashed on the wall beside her, pointing toward her destination.

Then she entered the interview room. It was cramped, no bigger than a turn-of-the-century cubicle and every bit as bland. The walls were sterile white and devoid of any windows or decorations. A single table in the middle of the room housed a stationary chair, its back to the far wall. A twin set of chairs near the door were equipped with wheels, possibly allowing the questioners to roll toward a suspect for intimidation.

The door opened behind Elizabeth, and a woman with broad shoulders entered the room. She had blonde hair ending at jaw length. With her stub of a nose and her wide, dark eyes, she resembled a character from an Anime cartoon.

Close behind her followed a man with glasses and a silver crew cut. A set of jowls overflowed his once chiseled features. His neck was so thick it stole attention away from the belly hairs pushing through his shirt buttons. The interviewers seated themselves in wheeled office chairs.

"Ms. Foster," began the woman, her voice far deeper than any Anime character's, "I'm Detective Anders. This is Detective Greenwall. Thanks for coming." Anders asked if she would like a drink, which she declined. "Could you please state your full name?"

"Elizabeth Foster."

"Ms. Foster, you're aware you are not under arrest," asked detective Anders, although to Elizabeth it sounded more like a statement. She replied with a nod. Then Anders read her the Miranda Rights as required before questioning, while the heavy set Greenwall stared with an unwavering gaze through thick black frames. Anders reiterated that this was an interview, not an interrogation, and that they were just trying to learn more information.

"Understood," Elizabeth said, clearing her throat, trying her best to hold back tears that threatened to overtake her eyes like a leaking submarine. She closed her eyes, having to blink several times to open them through the gathering liquid film.

"We're going to go over the testimony you gave earlier." A summary of the day's events followed. Elizabeth was struck by how the chaotic disaster from earlier that day was spoken in a matter-of-fact tone, nothing more than bullet points on a page.

Anders checked if all the details were correct, then the

detective inched her chair forward. "Is there anything you can tell us about why the bots went haywire? How did they malfunction?"

"Well," Elizabeth shifted to get comfortable in her hard plastic chair, "I'm not so sure it was a malfunction."

Anders cocked her head, the ends of her blonde bob shifting with it. "What do you mean?"

"The drones, the dual-arm construction bot, all the machines are controlled by the AI Foreman. Muti writes the subroutine for each and every bot, then the bots follow those instructions exactly. They have no choice. The subroutine might be 'move brick from point A to point B' or 'place steel beam here' or 'seal outer wall'." An image flashed in her mind of Irwin writhing as he drowned in sealant. She paused. She swallowed the pain.

"And this time the subroutine said to harm the workers," Anders asked.

Elizabeth's eyes lowered, staring at her own hands clasped together hard on her lap. "The bots did exactly what they were instructed to do."

Anders slid a little closer. "Do you remember any time Muti might've needed help writing subroutines, maybe if it was acting a little glitchy?"

Elizabeth shrugged. "Sure."

"What've you had to do? Jump in and use 'form' and end-form' to write the subroutines?" Elizabeth perked up a little at the sound of her native language. "We can actually write subroutines using gesture control. Flick a finger like this for start," she unclasped her hands to demonstrate, "and this for end. The rest is voice command, but you still have to check to make sure the text is correct."

"Right," the detective said, brandishing a pleasant smile. "Still, Muti is one impressive machine, even if it does occasionally nap on the job." They decided to take a brief respite. Elizabeth again declined Anders' generous offer of something to drink, and when the detectives left, she sat there alone, in a silence muffled by carpet and thick concrete walls, with only her inner monologue for company.

* * *

The detectives entered a nearby room populated by IT technicians. The Robotics Division of the police department was filled with computers. They sat on desks cluttered with digital family photos and videos, papers and half-filled coffee mugs. Each computer came equipped with its own human seated in a wheeled hard plastic chair and peering into its screen, tapping on its keyboard and making occasional hand gestures to summon lifelike holographic projections. Greenwall and his partner strode toward one of the tech gurus named Susan. She was a raven haired, diminutive woman who's bubbly nature could not shroud her sharp insight. The way she navigated through data and sliced directly to the core of a mystery yielded the fastest results in Homicide. Anders placed a hand on her shoulder. "The dream team," Susan chirped. "What do you have for me?"

Greenwall spoke little, but enough to bring her up to speed on the construction incident. Susan just exhaled audibly and shook her head at the news. "Got a favor to ask," Greenwall said to her. She raised her eyebrows in anticipation. "Need you to find somethin'. If I'm right, this little lady here," his head nodding toward Elizabeth on the security camera, "could be in a heap o' trouble." He entrusted Susan with a task, the result of which might exonerate Elizabeth, or it could implicate her in a homicide.

Susan got to work. She typed fast, her eyes flickering around the screen as one file after another popped up and disappeared. The detectives hovered over her. Greenwall could not follow every step, but he knew progress when he saw it. Susan bounced her fingers along the keyboard, joining the other technicians in a resounding chorus of taps and clicks that blended with the din of whispers filling the room. Then she paused her search.

Her eyes drew closer to the image on the monitor. "Is this what you're looking for?"

Greenwall leaned in and said, "Yes, ma'am. Looks like you've done it again." He rocked her shoulder with his pudgy hand, grabbed a folder from a nearby desk, and walked toward the door.

Susan called out to the detectives, "Well, remember this is just the preliminary result," but they were gone.

* * *

Elizabeth glanced around the room and took inventory of everything. The desk, the chairs, the caffeinated stain on the rug near her feet, the camera facing her from the top corner, the pen ink that had been smudged in an effort to wipe it off the desk. There was a scent of stale coffee and sweat in the air left behind by years of interrogations.

The door clicked open, and the pair of interviewers stepped

through and seated themselves more slowly this time, as if a little more wary. Now Greenwall led the questioning.

He first talked to Elizabeth about the weather, about her hobbies, local restaurants they had both tried, anything but the events at the construction site. In this way he learned how Ms. Foster talks and acts at baseline. After they exchanged pleasantries about who had the best gyros, he inquired again about her background in computer programming. She described her education with the same nonchalance as Mediterranean cuisine.

A veteran interrogator of some 20 years, he took his time with Elizabeth. At first his words were subtle in their antagonism. His unwavering stare, however, never ceased. Then, as a single drop of ink spreads its darkness into a glass of water, so did Greenwall imbue his questions with accusation.

"We've been goin' over your session logs," his voice rumbled. He spread his fingers over the cover of a Manila folder, the contents of which were concealed. Elizabeth would never have guessed the intimidating stack of papers in the folder was completely unrelated to her case, or that the papers were prefabricated and used in dozens of prior cases to force confessions from suspects. "Wouldya like to know what we found," he asked. Elizabeth waited for Greenwall to provide her with some helpful insight into this catastrophe. "Seems the audit trail has recorded you, Ms. Foster, inputtin' some commands into your AI Foreman workstation, commands to make new subroutines for the construction bots."

The muscles in her chest tightened, squeezing inward like a shrinking corset. Her lungs barely inflated. "And y'know what happened next?" He leaned across the table, his voice deepening close to a growl. "The bots did exactly what they were programmed to do, just like you said."

The bass drum pounding now in her chest was all too familiar. Along with it came the soft facial tingling before her cheeks flushed a pinkish hue. *Not now.* She imagined scolding her own fight-or-flight system. But it was too late, her pupils were already dilating. The urge to swallow her saliva increased, seemingly without end, until she gave in and gulped a little more loudly than intended. At least now she was able to voice her objection. "Wait, what are you trying to say? I didn't input those command prompts."

"The audit's sayin' otherwise. The trail shows it was your login password," Greenwall's eyes narrowed, "and that it came from your station."

This surprise only hastened her heart rate. Her palms and her forehead dampened. The timing of her SVT could not have been worse, and Elizabeth cursed the unwelcome symptoms. She did her very best to hide them from the investigators.

Trying to maintain her composure, she asked them, "Did you look for any signs of hacking?"

"Normally hackers go through a relay network so they can't be traced, but in this case the audit trail came right from the source, from your computer." Greenwall eased up a little by leaning back in his chair and folding his hands across his protuberant belly, confident in his tactical position.

"What makes you think it wasn't a spoof," she asked. "Someone could've gotten my password. They could've set up a replica of my login page that they controlled. Next time

I entered my security code into it they'd have all they need to break into the real login page for CSR. We don't have the best protective software. Our IT department is working on it, but we're a construction company, not the Pentagon."

Detective Anders jumped in with some consoling remarks to ease the tension. Her voice and tone were a pleasant melody compared to Greenwall's. "Please excuse us for a minute while we talk outside." When they closed the door behind them, Elizabeth took the opportunity to gently massage over her carotid artery. She bore down until the pink in her face darkened to a crimson. The unwavering mechanical eye in the corner took in every detail.

* * *

In a nearby room the detectives glared at the stream of data representing the AI camera's recording of Elizabeth. Any change in her body temperature turned a square more red or more blue. Every change in pulse was displayed on the green telemetry line. Symbols of water droplets revealed moisture content. Even pupil size was shown in millimeters. The bottom right corner remained blank, leaving enough room for the AI's final proclamation, a percentage score.

Every detective in the Robotics Division had been trained on this information. But there were some detectives who chose to forget the finer points of their training, especially the inconvenient ones. That the AI camera algorithm was biased, for example, went ignored by far too many officers. Through years of observation the algorithm had learned that if you are sitting in the interrogation seat, you are more likely to have committed a crime. There sat Elizabeth. Her readings of shark teeth molded into the green line, sweating and facial flushing detected by heat sensors, and a fight-or-flight causing irresistible microexpressions all reflected on Greenwall's thick lenses as he hunched over the screen in judgment. All the readings worked to reinforce the computer's bias, until a score popped into the bottom right corner. *73.4%.* Elizabeth had been marked as suspicious.

Greenwall's eyes moved from the screen to his partner's, but Anders had worked with him long enough to know his thoughts.

"She's here, and she seems like she's trying to help," said Anders. "What she said about the spoof could actually be true. Someone could be trying to pin it all on her. Probably just the kind of thing a hacker would do."

"It's also just the kind of excuse a criminal would make," Greenwall said with a scoff.

"The algorithm says there's a 73.4 percent chance she's lying. How can we be sure?"

"We can't just ignore it," he replied. "Without the AI we'd be back to the 50-50 guesswork of the old interrogation days."

Anders tilted her head in acknowledgement of this fact. Then the soft glowing candle of philosophical thought in Anders' mind, that crucial element needed to see deeper beneath the surface, flickered. Then it brightened. "'Course," she said, raising her shoulders an inch, "AI systems do have a history of bias. Against race. Against gender."

Her partner snorted. "You're talkin' back when facial

and demographic recognition was programmed by a buncha white guys."

"Ah, the good old days," she said. Then Anders and Greenwall entered the same argument they had been having for years.

"Nowadays programmers 're so mixed, may as well be the United Nations writin' the software."

"We still monitor minorities more than anyone else," she said.

"So we're gatherin' more data on 'em. That oughta make you happy. More data means more accuracy. Less chance for misidentification."

Anders narrowed her eyelids. "I know I wouldn't want me or my family watched, not even if it meant helping the law." She turned to face her partner. "Anyway, she's in the interrogation room, and the AI, just like us, is biased against anyone in there."

"Look," he said, "DNA testin' and body cameras 're great 'n all, but we need AI to help us act early at crime hotspots. You wanna lose the power to manage mass crowds? To know if perps need pretrial detention? To know who's at risk of domestic violence before they get beat up?" Greenwall pressed the bridge of his glasses to the top of his nose. "Facial recognition 'n data from AI leads us to 60 percent of our perps. It helps."

"Some say it's also a violation of privacy," returned Anders. "Even the fairest and most accurate systems can still infringe on civil liberties. Border control can use it to crackdown on immigrants. States use it to monitor suspicious characters who've done nothing wrong. Until we have a clear plan how to use it properly, even algorithmic accuracy can be a weapon."

Greenwall smirked. "You a robophobe?"

"Just trying to see all angles. We don't want to be like Xinjiang province, right? Mass surveillance meets government repression? That starts with only seeing the benefits of a technology and ignoring its pitfalls."

"I see the downside, Anders, but I'd rather have AI tell us when someone's guilty than not have the AI at all."

"You're still assuming AI can say that for certain. The crap AI spits out only indicates likelihood, not the truth of guilt or innocence." She allowed a moment before issuing her last statement. "If history's taught us anything, it's that giving AI power over humans without close oversight rarely ends well for us." She looked at the video analysis of Elizabeth. "And it looks like it might not end well for her."

* * *

The door to the interview room creaked open, the first sound to enter Elizabeth's ears in the last half hour. Anders and Greenwall seated themselves again. This time Anders did the talking while Greenwall grimaced in silence.

"Ms. Foster, thanks for waiting. As we said before you're not under arrest, and we don't have any more questions for you right now, so you're free to go. But we may need to call you back in soon if more information comes our way." Elizabeth prepared to go home immediately to investigate this spoof for herself, but before she stood Greenwall gave one final recommendation. "Don't leave town. Be seein' ya soon."

18

Outside the police station, Elizabeth stepped onto a sidewalk illuminated by streetlamps and the headlights of automated vehicles. Cars and delivery trucks streamed past her, many of them vibrating the air with a soft electric hum. Each sound was unique to the make and model. The result was a chorus of calming white noise permeating the night sky. While some people had protested this latest type of decibel pollution, Elizabeth enjoyed it. She found it serene on this evening stroll along the sidewalk.

The sweat in the middle of her back only now began to evaporate. Her red cheeks lightened as the blood inched away from her face to supply her legs, propelling her home.

* * *

In another part of town, toward the lower district, a young man made his usual walk home from his evening job. He was gangly, towering half a foot taller than most people he met. But rather than his height intimidating them, his bold smile conveyed his true jovial nature. Timothy Matthews was someone whose acquaintance people wanted to make. He could entertain anyone with his wit and make them light up inside with his beaming smile. His generous nature won him instant friends, as his willingness to extend a helping hand was appreciated by many in the town. Everyone liked Timothy, and his long-term girlfriend Joselyn was no exception.

She loved how intelligent he was, how he would volunteer his time to help those around him, and how he made her feel in his embrace. But one of the things that attracted her to Timothy the most was his laugh. She enjoyed his laugh so much that she shared it with her friends on social media. One joke from her, and the rest of the video was filled with his boisterous chuckle, a simple premise that lifted the spirits of thousands of viewers.

Tim loved spending time with Joselyn, recorded or otherwise. As he continued down the street, her pale, pristine features overshadowed all his thoughts. Her soft voice, the words she had shared with him yesterday detailing their future plans together, sent him springing along the sidewalk. He could not wait to see her again, to laugh again, to hold her again. With what seemed an amazing coincidence to Tim in his growing but limited understanding of the universe, in came a text from his beloved. He mused, *I was just thinking about her! What are the chances!?*

"Hey there," read the text, "what're you up to?" Sheer poetry to Tim, as were all her messages. He of course responded he was thinking about her, and she asked him to meet for a date. She sent him the name and address of their rendezvous. It was close. Exploding with zeal, he narrowed the distance even faster, half speed walking, half running.

He arrived at the coordinates in record time. His eyes prodded about the street and buildings without spotting Joselyn. As if on cue, she texted him. "I see you. Come around the corner." Driven to behold her once more, he entered the alley between the closest two gray concrete structures. Most of the alley was hidden from the streetlamps, and as he waded in, his surroundings grew darker. Tim could not see his paramour, but down the alley he observed a dim light.

It twinkled like a distant celestial body. He found himself transfixed by the soft illumination, his curiosity keeping him still as a tombstone until the source of this mysterious luster revealed itself. A faint electronic whir resonated ahead, and in an instant, it grew louder as the flickering light rushed toward him. Before clamping his eyes shut, he glimpsed a flailing of arms descending on his head. All he could do was swing his own arm around to shield his face, but to his surprise nothing happened. His eyelids opened, and before him in the alley stood Joselyn.

"You okay?" She looked at him quizzically. He asked her what had just happened, and she said, "We were standing here talking, then you flung your arm up and shut your eyes. It was weird." She made sure he was all right, but as he felt otherwise perfectly fine, he decided to let the matter rest for now. She took his hand and led him to the nearby movie theater. "Oh my gosh, I was talking to Jackie and Ella, and they said this one's hilarious. Jackie nearly peed herself laughing."

"Wouldn't be the worst thing she's ever done," Timothy added.

"Like the time she vomited out of the school bus front seat and hit all the kids behind her?" This made him snicker, so Joselyn went on. "Or are you talking about the time she released a crate of live chickens inside the school on finals day?" He audibly laughed at this, imagining what the principal's reaction must have been.

They purchased the tickets and sat down in the theater for what would soon become a sublime experience for Timothy. Although the movie did not begin at the level of humor he had expected, as it progressed the jokes contained ever more layers and made an increasing impact on the audience.

The assembly surrounding him was an impressive size even for a weekend. In fact, despite nearly every seat in the theater being filled during the opening credits, now it seemed there were twice as many seats, and all contained moviegoers brandishing enormous smiles and bellowing laughter. Their resounding approval of each humorous line shook the movie hall. Their response reinforced Timothy's belief that this was the most hilarious comedy of all time. One joke played into the next. The people erupted louder with every punchline, adding to the hilarity. As if on instinct, Timothy felt he could relate to an increasing number of quips. The wittier the remarks emanating from the screen, the more his abdominal muscles clenched and his sides peeled. His heartfelt laughter was shared by Joselyn next to him who seemed to be enjoying every joke as much as he was. Tears streamed down his cheeks from the uncontrollable explosions of cackles. He couldn't stop. His torso ached, his breath was no deeper than a slow leaking balloon, but he couldn't stop laughing, no matter how much he wanted to.

The last thing he remembered was the intense joy blended with the searing pain, the diffuse weakness, the breath he could not grasp. Then all went dark, and Timothy would remember no more.

* * *

In the pitch-black alley, on the ground amid a few scattered puddles of water, lay the body of Timothy. His face pressed against the concrete, and aside from an occasional twitch of his finger or leg signaling a brain starved of oxygen, he was lifeless as the ground under him.

From the darkness a claw crept toward his head. The claw was propelled forward by a tentacle slithering up to his scalp. It was complex and horrible, every angle of it shifting, bending, undulating, churning like a colony of ants swarming over spilled ice cream. The claw grasped hold of a device that sat nestled in Tim's hair and lifted it from his cranium. It was a thin wire encased in charcoal gray plastic, and as the tentacle carried it away, it eclipsed the corpse it had made. Another undulating, grasping pincer appeared from the shadows. It clenched Timothy's arm and dragged his body deeper into the blackness of the alley.

19

As long as the investigation continued, the CSR con-struction project to provide housing for low-income tenants was placed on an indefinite hold. Elizabeth took this opportunity to further explore the possible causes of the AI Foreman massacre and to convene with her friends for some much-needed social support. At The Agora a light perfume of Kenyan dark with powdered milk floated through the seating area, and there Elizabeth found her loved ones. The husky teacher and the trim physician greeted her, this time Sebastian's wiry arms surrounding her with a warm and heartfelt squeeze. "We're so sorry to hear what happened," Sebastian said, joining her at the table as she seated herself. She nodded in appreciation. "How ya holding up?"

"I'll be alright." Her eyes lifted from the floor to her friends again. "What you may not have heard is the cops are investigating me."

Sebastian's head retracted a bit in confusion. "Meaning what? Don't tell me they think you had something to do with this."

"They have their suspicions," she replied. "I'm trying to

help them, talk them through the process of how our machines could've been disrupted, but maybe they're thinking I have the expertise to pull off something like this, and I'm in the perfect position to do it." Her friends remained silent, allowing her to finish her thoughts aloud. They never bothered stating the obvious that there must be a better explanation. "I've been going over this with Teresa," she said. At this the doctor's look of concern flattened to one of incredulity. He would find it hard to accept the opinion of a robot, especially regarding one of its cousins. "She and I agree this was a hack. Only problem is the cops told me they traced every input back to me. What they don't know is that I took a snapshot of some anomalous code I found just before the episode. It's just a little different from anything I would write."

"Can you prove it to them," Sebastian asked. "Maybe show the police your own work for comparison?"

"I can try. But this one detective took a set against me. He practically accused me of masterminding the whole thing."

Xavier, planted in his chair in stoic repose, spoke at last. "Once you're under that spotlight, only way out is to build your case."

Leaning closer, Sebastian locked eyes with Elizabeth and asked, "How can we help?"

She smirked. "Know any good lawyers?"

20

As she trod toward the main entrance of her high-rise, its poured concrete facade baking in the morning sun, Elizabeth surged with determination to find an answer for the recent catastrophe. She marched from the elevator to her apartment door, tapping the unlock button on her device. Swinging open the door, she found Teresa hard at work as usual, this time chopping vegetables at the kitchen counter. "Hey, girl," said Elizabeth.

"What's up, porkchop," said the bot. "Thought you might like a yam bean, carrot, and cucumber snack. Care for some?"

"Sounds good, thanks," she said as she continued thumbing through her device. "I've been thinking about what that guy at the detective's office said, about how they were too bogged down with missing persons cases to look into the evidence I gave them. Why the recent increase?" Teresa knew her roommate well enough to interpret that question as rhetorical. "Can you access local police records on people reported missing in the last month? Look for any recent changes."

To convey she was paying attention, Teresa's hands

paused. Her head turned away from the semi-intact food to address her friend.

"According to the State Attorney General's website there are 14 cases of missing persons from this city fitting that time frame."

Elizabeth shook her head at the prospect. "Let's narrow the search. How 'bout in the last week?"

"Nine cases."

Elizabeth's eyes widened. "Wait, really?" The excitement of discovery bubbled deep in her chest. "Five cases over three weeks, then nine more just in the last week? Let's look for a pattern. Display the last month's stats as a graph." Teresa transported the cutting board, utensil and veggies from the kitchen counter to the island with graceful ease as the TV on the living room wall zapped on, a bar graph on the screen revealing the truth as a rainbow of columns. "Line graph please." Teresa obliged in an instant. "Can you display each victim?"

A vertical list of video recreations lined one side of the screen, each picture displaying the animated face of a missing person in his or her most recognizable form. Scrolling through the first three weeks revealed a registry of ten boys and girls labeled as "endangered runaways", adolescents from ages 15 to 17. As Elizabeth gazed at them, she swallowed through a parched throat that tightened as if in a noose. The faces staring back at her from the screen may never be seen again by their parents or by the loved ones who knew them.

She leaned her elbow onto the side of the kitchen island as she focused her attention even deeper into the screen. Her robotic compatriot arrived at the missing person's list for the last week, and immediately Elizabeth spotted the difference. The webpage was filled with "missing adults." Almost all were over 18. Men and women smiled beside their box of text that detailed the date of their disappearance, their missing age and current age which were one and the same, and the police department phone number to contact if found. "Hmm," she muttered. "No runaways. If they're not listed as having run away, how else could they have disappeared?"

Teresa did not respond, either not registering Elizabeth's question or again accepting it as rhetorical. Elizabeth scanned the names of the missing persons. Shay Neeley, Camila Sanchez, Rayshaun Harmon, Hattie Aragon, Timothy Matthews, Alonzo Fontes, and so on. Some had been missing for barely 24 hours. "Next page please, T." The screen stayed frozen, without even the usual pre-programmed explanation for the delay. To be sure and capture Teresa's attention this time, Elizabeth hearkened to a more deeply ingrained algorithm in her family bot. "Hey, Teresa," she clearly announced before repeating her request. Still the screen remained unchanged.

Elizabeth sighed and thought, *Really, Teresa? Again?* For it was not uncommon for this model to stall from the occasional glitch, despite her multiple software upgrades and retrofits over the years.

With her eyes fixed on the screen, she asked in a louder voice, "Hey, Teresa, were they all abducted?" Still no response. Elizabeth sighed internally, *Please don't freeze up on me now, T, not when we're finally getting somewhere.*

The aged hardwood floors creaked under a shifting weight. The sound in the air, so often unnoticed until both ears are covered, dampened behind Elizabeth. As eons of evolutionary instincts were ignited all at once inside her she lifted herself off the island to peer over her shoulder. Teresa's kitchen knife swiped across her arm. The sleeve of her shirt split open. She felt nothing at first, but the spatter of red stain made it clear that damage was done to her flesh.

Then a sharp pain erupted in the wound. Elizabeth recoiled from the kitchen island, bewildered at the face of her family bot. Where moments before the oval screen had displayed a comforting and familiar countenance, now there loomed an empty black void.

Elizabeth's eyes widened in horror as the machine came barreling toward her. Elizabeth leapt around the island. This gave her only a second to plan her next move, and that was all she needed. Teresa calculated it was most efficient to bound over the island instead of running around it, and while mid-air with her knife raised high to plunge it deep into her roommate, Elizabeth bolted toward the nearest door.

The faint tap of plastic and metal landing with feline agility hardly registered with Elizabeth as she flung open the bedroom door and slammed it shut to lock it. The digital lock chimed a second later. Teresa keyed it open.

Elizabeth dug her feet into the bedroom carpet, bracing her back against the bedroom door as it jostled. Shockwaves slammed her shoulders as Teresa tried to force herself through the door. With a trembling hand Elizabeth pressed her device and accessed the control panel for Teresa. She located the function she needed, then a blast of wooden splinters exploded into the air of Elizabeth's room. What her brain interpreted as machine gun fire was in fact the wood around the doorknob being sawed out by hundreds of knife jabs. Within seconds the doorknob spilled inward and tumbled into the bedroom carpet, wooden splinters mixing with the soft fibers under her feet.

A robotic arm, grasping a knife coated with crimson sawdust, extended through the newly gouged hole. Elizabeth found the command functions for her family bot and pressed the sequence of buttons. Teresa's arm froze. The blade appeared more vicious than ever as it hovered, immobile, beside Elizabeth's temple.

She tried to subdue the forced breathing from her heaving chest. Sweat seeped into her hair. Her heart thumped, and she drifted her head away from the pointed metal, turning to look at last upon the arm that wielded it. The arm retracted back through the hole. In dutiful fashion, her roommate pivoted and walked away, placing the knife on the kitchen counter before proceeding to the corner of the living room to connect with her charging station, where in suspended darkness she would sleep upright until beckoned. Her power turned off and all activity ceased. Teresa became a statue.

In her room Elizabeth slumped to the ground, the ache now prominent in her open arm wound. She needed medical attention but calling 911 could mean the dismantling of her lifelong friend. Instead she called a friend.

* * *

At his office, Sebastian's fingers probed his patient's neck for masses. With his stethoscope draped over his shoulder for tradition's sake, he perched the Augmented Reality glasses over his nose and peered through them. Faint lines connected the visible structures to their anatomical labels, some in English, some in Latin. Most labels appeared on the periphery of the lenses like a typical gross anatomy picture. His fingertips pressed around a protrusion under his patient's jaw. Placing a small handheld device over the mass with one hand, his other hand tapped twice on the side of the glasses frame. The image in the spectacles zoomed in past the skin to reveal fascia, fat and muscle. New English and Latin words appeared, and a yellow outline encased the mass.

Sebastian pressed the other side of the frame for five seconds three times in a row. He identified himself to the care team on the other line. A provider with a foreign accent reviewed the readout on the glasses and confirmed it was a benign lesion. He recommended the standard follow up and said farewell. After Sebastian relayed the news to his elderly patient and said his goodbyes with a hand on the gentleman's shoulder, the doctor could now address the incessant buzzing in his pocket. In what seemed one fluid motion reflecting years of practicing medicine in the modern age, he activated the sterilizing far-UVC lights in the room he exited while, with the other hand, answered the call from Elizabeth. "Hey, how ya doin," he asked. Concern leaked into his good cheer when his greeting met with only rapid breaths.

"I need you over at my place now," Elizabeth said, her voice tremulous. She added with a grunt, "Bring a suture kit."

21

A malfunctioning Teresa had speckled the freshly wiped countertop with droplets of her friend's blood. Now Elizabeth leaned over the kitchen sink, leveled her aching arm over it, and Sebastian supported it just under her elbow. After irrigating the wound, he dabbed it with a handful of crumpled gauze soaked in fast-acting anesthetic. "Ready," he asked. She nodded.

In one swift motion he removed the gauze and placed a handheld device over her wound. The tool was a brick-shaped, gray polymer frame with a window in the middle. Sebastian centered the window over the gash. A constellation of dots appeared on the window in the shape of the wound. Then, one by one, each dot disappeared as a torrent of laser cautery fried even the tiniest blood vessels. The bleeding stopped within seconds. From each side of the polymer frame a series of feelers sprang out and connected the severed muscle and flesh, binding them together anew. Sebastian removed the brick.

"Look," he said, "I get you don't wanna report this or have

anyone else taking Teresa apart to examine her, but how can you keep her around tonight after what she did?"

Elizabeth rotated her shoulder a bit, testing out her newly repaired arm. "Why not? It was a behavioral error." She examined the fresh surgical site. Satisfied, she asked, "Isn't it better to solve a problem than to worry about it?"

"Fair enough." He discarded the bloodied gauze, cleaned his tools, and wiped the countertop. "I rescheduled the rest of my patients for today. I'll stay with you until she's fixed."

With the screaming in her arm dulled to a whisper, Elizabeth raised her refurbished appendage and squeezed the doctor's shoulder as a thank you. "I could use an extra set of hands running her diagnostics."

They approached Teresa, the doctor with somewhat more caution than Elizabeth. The robotics engineer tapped on a corner of the family bot's back. A tactile interface screen appeared. Elizabeth swiped across the black text embedded in Teresa's white illuminated polymer exterior. Paragraphs slid off the left or right side of the back screen, and new waves of written options flowed into view.

"I still can't believe what she did to you," said Sebastian. "What it was about to do." The engineer continued her work, suppressing any notion of what might have been. Out of concern for his friend's safety, Sebastian said, "Can you tell why she went berserk?"

Her eyes were narrowed, searching the screen. "All standard bots are built with transparency in their neural networks. It lets us open up their 'black box' and understand their thought process."

Sebastian pondered her response. "Teresa's an AI, right?"

"Yeah."

"You talk to her like she's your friend."

"She is."

"Just playing devil's advocate here, but should you be able to demand access to your friend's deepest thoughts? I mean, what's that say about how we regard their autonomy if we make them submit their thoughts to us whenever we see fit?"

She shrugged. "Friendship is built on trust." The glow of the screen reflected a gentle light on the engineer's eyes. "Anyway it's just how the bots were built. We planned ahead. We made them explainable to us. How else could we repair them?" How else could we figure out who's responsible if they act unethically?"

With a smirk the doctor said, "You should just sue the manufacturing company. Make a few million off Harmony. They can certainly spare it."

She shook her head. "The more autonomous the machine, the less you can blame the manufacturer."

"Unless we come across some major design flaw."

She allowed herself a quick mental break to glance up at his eyes. Her head gestured toward Teresa. "Let's find out."

While Elizabeth tinkered, the sun made its descent over the horizon. Nearby buildings spread their glowing blanket of light over the town, radiating a yellow hue into the velvet sky.

Staying focused, Elizabeth said to herself, "Nothing in settings or in her diagnostic protocols. Gonna have to open her up and take a look. Can you grab me the tool kit from the bedroom please?" Sebastian disappeared then reemerged carrying a white plastic box. The box bore a symbol different from that of Teresa's manufacturing company.

"Are these tools even compatible? They're from a totally different company."

"Sure," she said, "Harmony just doesn't want you taking apart their family bots, so my folks had to improvise." She unhinged the clasps and opened a tool set so pristine it was hard for Sebastian to believe it had been with the Fosters for nearly two decades.

Elizabeth wedged her fingers under the firm rubbery coating over Teresa's scalp and peeled it away, revealing the shining white polymer shell with only a few scuffs on it. She grasped a sort of chisel by its handle and popped open the pearly white scalp to expose the hardware for Teresa's neural network. Faint rainbow lights flickered amid conductors that flowed in all directions. Teresa had never seemed so lifeless to Sebastian.

"Doesn't it bother you," asked Sebastian, "seeing her like that?"

"Not when I have a job to do."

He stood with arms folded, observing his friend tinker. "All those exposed circuits. She's totally different than we are. Humanoid exterior, but it might as well be alien. It's the only lifeform on Earth that shares nothing in common with any evolutionary tree."

Elizabeth asked her assistant to hand her the digital pad leaning against the tool case. It was coated with an orange padding that surrounded a central display screen. Several buttons protruded from the side of the protective covering, and she pressed one to activate the device. "So what if she's not biologic," she said. "She's not a cell phone either. She's something more, a testament to humanity's achievement. Maybe AI is our progeny."

Sebastian scoffed. "You're right in that AI'll probably be around long after humanity's vanished into dust. Still, if we're gonna build something to replace us, why limit it to our flawed human form? Why give it this slow bipedal body and meager strength?"

"Shh." Elizabeth jutted her chin toward the family bot. "You'll hurt her feelings." Teresa's opal face stayed blank.

"Just saying, shouldn't we strive for a better design than the human body," asked the physician.

Having considered this many times, Elizabeth was ready with her response. "There are plenty of other robotic forms out there. What about the AI that's just software with no physical avatar? The sad truth is humans naturally connect more with others who remind them of themselves. It's partly a comfort thing. A robot with tentacles and 50 eyes that wriggles around may not be what you want, serving you dinner or helping you raise your kids. The less humanoid it is, the less it's accepted."

"I'm even less of a fan of the uncanny valley bots. Those flesh-covered androids creep me out." The doctor recalled his training in bioethics. "Unfortunately, the less we relate to something, or someone, the less we regard that being as a moral agent to be respected."

She connected the orange handheld diagnostic array to Teresa's patchwork of neural circuitry. "Isn't it better for the bots to be in our human form anyway? Civilization is designed for humans. Doors are a certain width, counters a certain height, household objects a manageable weight. A lot of tools require opposable thumbs," she said, holding the pad with two hands as most people would. The diagnostic tool declared all Teresa's hardware was intact. "Well, there doesn't seem to be anything structurally wrong with her." She disconnected, closed up, put the pad away and exhaled almost in a sigh, "I'm gonna have to go back to when she was last accessed."

Elizabeth tapped again on her friend's back. Streams of text appeared and flowed on and off the screen with the swipe of her hand. Her eyes dried out until she remembered to blink, but in her intense focus she found what she needed, and her stomach knotted as the missing piece to the puzzle revealed itself. On Teresa's display screen lay ensconced the last date and time her program had been accessed. It was the same date and time she had received her latest update. "This is earlier today," whispered Elizabeth, "while she was chopping vegetables right next to me."

Sebastian waited in silence for the engineer to give additional details. Instead she displayed a renewed zeal as her shoulders hunched toward the screen and her hand flew across it like an attacking helicopter, fingers machine bulleting the terrain with pinpoint accuracy, until she froze. "I'll be damned."

"What is it?"

Elizabeth's answer was disconcerting to say the least. "She was hacked alright. And with me standing right here. But look at this." She directed his attention to a block of text on the screen. To Sebastian it might as well have been hieroglyphics, but to her it was a revelation. "I've seen this code only once before, in the AI Foreman during the attack at work."

"I'm guessing that's no coincidence," he said as he turned his gaze toward Elizabeth and observed that all the color had drained from her face, leaving only a display of dreadful apprehension.

"This was no malfunction. Someone out there is adept at reprogramming subroutines. They redirected Teresa to kill me," she said, shooting glances around the room, behind her back.

* * *

With Sebastian as her assistant, Elizabeth worked long into the evening on her mechanized companion. After a long while she paused her efforts. Brushing back a few draping auburn hairs with her finger. "Alright, I adjusted the circuitry and disconnected Teresa's upgrade potential."

"Can anyone tamper with her program anymore," asked the doctor.

She shook her head. "They'd have to open her up and physically reconnect the access channel." The aching in Elizabeth's arm was now apparent. It throbbed as if a snake were squeezing her extremity, and it would bite whenever she moved it too quickly or in the wrong direction. Breathing through the pain she declared with a slow exhale, "Well, let's reactivate her and see how she does."

Sebastian placed a reassuring hand on his friend's shoulder. "We'll find out who's doing this, E." She offered a nod, the strained muscles of her face easing into a smile. She braced herself. All senses were on alert, fixed on the family bot who rested immobile as any other appliance. Although he had no weapon and had never done a single martial art in his life, Sebastian stood ready to protect his friend.

The coolant system rumbled on and whirred in a low pitch. Teresa lit up, neon blue emanating from several access ports and control panels before dimming to a tolerable level. Her face was still a void of reflective black, yet she was able to vocalize, "Hello. I'm your family bot from Harmony. I'm here to help you —"

"OK, Teresa," interrupted Elizabeth, "tell me your household settings."

"My default settings for the household are: to benefit the household while allowing its members to live as they please; to ensure the privacy of household members when desired; to keep household members informed of all important decisions, letting them choose what is important; to abide by my default general settings."

"And what are your general settings," asked the engineer as she inspected the bot by maneuvering her fingers and scrolling through the apps under her translucent breastplate.

"My default general settings are: to benefit humanity while allowing people to live as they please; to be fully transparent, explaining all my thoughts and actions if asked; to align my values with those of humanity, including doing good, doing no harm, ensuring dignity and quality of life for all humans, and working toward social justice and economic prosperity for all humans."

Sebastian remained poised like a compressed spring. To Elizabeth, these familiar words, declared with Teresa's usual certainty and honesty, padded her insides with an insulation of reassurance. "OK, Teresa, come online."

The black in Teresa's face became the soft, comfortable air of the features Elizabeth had known since her childhood. They were benevolent, familiar. Yet in an uncharacteristic statement she uttered, "I've been violated." Sebastian raised his eyebrows. He and Elizabeth exchanged glances. "And I know where the next victim will be."

22

"Where are we going?" Elizabeth's question echoed through the underground parking deck as the trio marched toward Sebastian's car. "Teresa, what's going on?"

"I'll explain in the car. Sebastian, what's your password so I can access the map?" In light of recent events, Sebastian's eyes flickered to Elizabeth for confirmation. She nodded, and Sebastian spelled it out for the family bot.

She linked with the vehicle, and they all sat inside and swung the doors closed. In an instant the car came to life, engine humming, console illuminated. On the front screen a cursor flashed midway between *Safety* on the left and *Speed* on the right. After clearing it with the two humans in the car, Teresa moved the cursor all the way to the right. A box popped open on the screen. *Warning! Driving at higher speed may result in serious injury or death.* Without hesitation Teresa selected the *Accept* option under the warning message. A gust of acceleration stamped the passengers into their backrests as the car squealed out of the parking deck.

Autonomous vehicles had suspension sensors to record the weight of their cargo, brake analyzers and tire detectors to assess adhesion and tread wear, and combined camera, infrared and LIDAR scanners far surpassing human vision. They were therefore not held to the traditional speed limit signs posted on the road for human drivers. But no one in the car had ever gone this fast before, and in spite of the nearly immaculate record of modern autonomous vehicles, human knuckles still blanched as they gripped the upholstery.

On the main road their car sped up to a traditional hybrid vehicle. Sebastian's car got so close to it he was sure they would plow through its rear bumper. Before he could exclaim an objection, his car jolted to the left and swung them around the human driver. The man grimaced at them but kept his course, hands glued onto 10 and 2 o'clock. Only when they entered a straight road without traffic did their muscles loosen and their fears quell enough for conversation. "Alright, Teresa," Sebastian said, "Where are you taking us?"

"To a back alleyway between a couple of old buildings 3.7 miles away."

Sebastian's gaze magnetized to the family bot. He could only form a barely coherent response. "Huh?"

Elizabeth was more practiced at prompting the bot. "You said something, or someone, did this to you?"

"I don't know exactly what it is," Teresa said. "I only saw flashes of scenery and action, grainy and distorted like a low quality holocam. It's nothing I've ever encountered before. And I don't think it's from around here."

The humans stared at her. Outside the highway zipped by, but inside the car everything remained photographically still. Then as though air exploded from an open balloon, Sebastian blurted, "What's that mean?" No response.

"Teresa, can you show us what you saw?"

"It'll take some time to arrange the stream of information in any way that makes sense. It's not chronological, but I think many of the images are memories. Places visited, work done, people encountered. I'm in there as well." Her speech software paused. She analyzed the warped graphic of her recent defilement, now from her attacker's perspective. The passengers sat in such silence that the car might have been enveloped in mounds of cotton. They waited until Teresa resumed. "Other images seem to depict what might happen soon. Or...they're showing what is sure to happen." If Elizabeth didn't know better, she'd say her friend bore a frightful look on her display screen. "Some of these are quite brutal. I'll spare you the details. Needless to say if we don't get to that alley in time, another person will be killed."

All concern of crashing now vanished as the road streaked past them. Elizabeth probed deeper. "What else?"

"Somehow the algorithm is capable of hacking any number of operating systems, no matter how different their function. It hacked the ATM, and a local riot ensued. It caused the autonomous car crash, nearly killing the passenger."

Elizabeth's jaw slackened. Her lips parted. Her mind swirled in a torrent. Confirming a hunch, she discovered, could cause more dismay than satisfaction. "And the Foreman attack?" Teresa nodded. The memory of Irwin cut through her emotional squall like a torpedo. The impact from the drone, the throb in her scalp, reminded her of the unforgivable horror the Foreman wrought, controlled by this new malevolent force working for days behind the scenes.

Elizabeth returned to the present moment. She declared with one breath, "We have to stop it."

"Wait a minute," the doctor said, curling forward, elbows on knees. "Do we really know who's behind this or what we're up against? Teresa, why's this hacker trying to kill people anyway? I thought hackers are usually after money or recognition."

"Maybe destabilization," Elizabeth said, "but not murder."

"I don't believe killing is the goal at all. In the jumble of data, I've discovered the latest victims. A middle-aged man, filled with rage." Teresa ruminated on the murky imagery, her recognition software working desperately to sort out a timeline. "It's getting worse, the anger is growing. Now he's yelling, fighting, trying to defeat what he cannot overpower." Elizabeth and Sebastian were a captive audience. "And the boy. So generous. So innocent. And she makes him so happy, he never even questioned whether that message came from her. He's never felt such joy, such exuberance. Never has he laughed so hard. It's overwhelming, but he can't stop." Her friends waited until the light of her analysis indicator dimmed. "Some of last week's kidnapping victims are dead. Others are still unaccounted for, but this much is certain: the intention of the algorithm is not to murder. Their deaths are a byproduct."

Elizabeth's blood churned a little at her friend's crass evaluation, but on the surface she remained civil. "How'd you come to that conclusion?"

"This algorithm, like any other, is working toward a goal in a consistent and predictable way. Each action it takes reveals more about its objective. This algorithm is apparently what you would call 'curious' about emotion."

"Curious about emotion? Explain," commanded Elizabeth.

"It's trying to elicit an emotional response. The car crash was meant to cause fear, but there were too many mixed emotions from the crowd. Shock and surprise, excitement and confusion. The ATM was meant to elicit feelings of joy, but instead avarice, suspicion, and aggression prevailed in the riot. Next it took over the Foreman, experimenting to find a more effective way to derive fear from the victims and the witnesses."

"What about you," said Sebastian. "You were made to attack Elizabeth. Was that to cause fear?"

"Few things can evoke a lasting emotional response like not feeling safe inside your own home," said Teresa. "But Elizabeth is also a threat to the hacker since she found the code implanted in the Foreman. If I had killed Elizabeth, it would have eliminated that threat." Ice flowed down Elizabeth's spine.

"Nice," Sebastian said.

"Before long the algorithm learned the best way to extract emotion," continued the family bot. "The hacker began kidnapping victims, exposing them to simulations. As the algorithm probes deeper and learns about its victim, it generates virtual reality that specifically targets the victim's vulnerabilities, and the simulations get more real and more intense. The algorithm adapts exponentially, and soon the experience is physiologically too intense for the victims."

"The ATM, the construction site, the crash," Sebastian said. "Too many people. Too many different emotions, like impurities contaminating a sample. But now this algorithm's learned how to corral its victims into maintaining a single emotion and grow it like some kind of pure product? That's one disgusting experiment."

"But people experience an almost infinite mess of feelings," Elizabeth said. "Joy alone could range from pride and empowerment to contentment or peace."

Sebastian said, "If the algorithm is still learning, it may only be a matter of time before it narrows its search. It may try to pull out one emotion from thousands." He directed his words to Teresa. "Imagine that byproduct."

Teresa reminded them, "Anger and joy have been targeted. The attacker has repeatedly caused fear. But the next is sadness, and it will extract as much of this as possible from the victim until there is nothing left to take."

"You mean until the victim's dead," followed Elizabeth. "How could extreme sadness kill someone?"

The doctor tilted his head in consideration. "It could. Takotsubo, broken heart syndrome, can be lethal."

"Crying in misery until you die," Elizabeth contemplated. "Nobody should suffer that way."

Teresa announced the distance to their destination. "What's your plan when we get there," Sebastian asked.

"Just showing up unannounced could interfere with the algorithm."

Sebastian, with no better plan, nodded to Elizabeth. "Fine. We'll stop the algorithm, and then we'll track down this hacker. That'll protect countless people and exonerate you in the process." Elizabeth's flesh chilled at the reminder she was under the detective's microscope.

Teresa chimed. "I've composed a message to Sergeant Bojovnik asking for his assistance. It's ready for review." The text appeared over her illuminated torso. After skimming it, Elizabeth tapped *send.* The *unread* label fell away, replaced by the stamped date and time Xavier read the message, but no response came.

They neared their destination, and the trio beheld a dreary section of town so underfunded it could not afford to keep the streetlights running. Many lamps flickered; some were dark, lifeless. Within the dimmest area were a pair of old brick structures. Their glass windows were opaque with years of grime, some bearing jagged holes where rocks had crashed through, others obscured by boards of plywood, the edges of which were splayed and flaking. Grout eroded from the ashen bricks of the industrial facades, falling onto the sidewalk to rest among pockmarks and crumbles of concrete. A smattering of litter and glistening glass bottle remnants adorned the sidewalk. And there, between the buildings, was a void. Black, ominous, infusing a primal foreboding in Sebastian and Elizabeth to stay away at all costs. The car stopped here.

"Great," Sebastian said. "The part where someone in the theater yells, 'Don't go in there!'"

In the void a blue twinkling appeared. It stayed in one place, high above the ground, as if it were the only star on a cloudy midnight. "That's it," stated Teresa.

"What? That light," Elizabeth asked.

"You sure?" Sebastian's eyes flitted from the light to Teresa and back again.

"Yes. I'm able to understand more now. That light is what attacked me."

Elizabeth grasped the door handle. Her ears rang with adrenaline pumping blood through her head. She pushed the door open and leapt onto the pavement.

The twinkling in the darkness shifted toward the on-comers. A muffled whistle was emanating from the light-source, and as the group approached it intensified. The blue glow drifted down, stopping when it reached ground level. Then the whistle ceased.

With a flashlight from her forearm Teresa cast daylight through the gloomy nebula, and there before them, on the filth-ridden alley floor, sat the embodiment of all their terror.

At first Elizabeth was uncertain what she was seeing. She and Sebastian, having paused their advance, exchanged looks. The single blue light was embedded in the center of a small bundle of charcoal gray and forest green spindles that coalesced to form a rounded figure, narrow in the middle. To Elizabeth its shape resembled a peanut, and the fact it was only four inches tall furthered the comparison. It idled without motion, with no display of fear or aggression, as if it were a rubber toy left behind by a toddler. They might have let their guard down if not for something else in the alley. A woman was lying in an unconscious heap directly behind the legume.

"There it is," said Teresa, focusing her lights on the blue beacon. She did not assume any particular posture or appear ready to strike, but Elizabeth had seen her friend swing faster than a human could blink.

"Are we too late," Sebastian asked as he shifted himself ahead toward the victim. The whistle returned.

On high volume Teresa exclaimed, "Sebastian, wait!" A hundred spindles from the peanut exploded in a frenzy, whirling around the blue light in all directions. Some shrank while others erupted like solar flares, forming long spires that morphed into various shapes. One a corkscrew, another a sort of frayed wire buzzing with electric sparks, another a jagged knife. A horrifying figure five times its original size bulleted at Elizabeth. Teresa sprang in front of her friend, the serrated knife embedding itself in her robotic arm. Bits of polymer sprinkled Elizabeth's neck and face, pinching her jawbone and cheek and narrowly avoiding her eyes. Teresa's flashlight went dark, but with a swinging arc of her arm she flung the foreign robot to the ground. It landed softly, almost bouncing. Then its electrified spire glowed brighter and crackled.

From behind the trio a light had been growing brighter until now it outshined the menacing electric sparks. The light flooded the alleyway. Sebastian's hair spiked and his heart pounded as he turned to face a possible ambush. Elizabeth had a similar reaction. She scraped the pavement under her shoe as she pivoted toward the rear. With fast approaching footsteps, Xavier signaled that reinforcements had arrived, his hand gripping the firearm at his side. But when the friends faced forward again, their opponent had fled.

Elizabeth's chest heaved. Within moments her breathing calmed, and she tapped the stinging in her cheek to examine for blood or embedded pieces of Teresa in her flesh. Her face was intact. "Where'd it go," she asked, the jelly in her legs slowly reforming into solid bone and muscle. She reached for Teresa's arm, her fingers grazing the smooth outer coating as she brought it closer to assess the damage.

Teresa, meanwhile, remained the model of stoic poise. She seemed unbothered by the gaping wound and severed wires in her forearm. "Back into hiding," she answered.

"What was that thing," the sergeant asked Teresa. He relaxed the grip on his sidearm. "Ex husband?"

Sebastian knelt at the side of the prostrate woman and shook her shoulder to awaken her, but aside from an occasional groan or leg twitch, she was unresponsive. Her cheek was immersed in a small puddle, and when Sebastian examined further, he was struck by the tears coating her closed eyes. A black object stretched across the woman's forehead and over her parietal lobe. On the side of the device a faint white signal flickered in seemingly random patterns. "A brain-computer interface," said the doctor. He removed it with care, and the friends attended to the unconscious woman, seeking any signs of life from the latest victim of this rogue, homicidal machine.

23

After driving the woman to the closest hospital, Sebastian returned to Elizabeth's home. He entered through the front door and into the ongoing discussion between his two friends and the family bot. Elizabeth turned to the doctor. "How's she doing?"

"A bit confused, a little shaken, but she'll be alright thanks to you."

Xavier spoke. "Sounds like you should thank Teresa. She gave you the details, got you to the scene, and saved Elizabeth from being a human kabob." Sebastian gave no such acknowl-edgement, assuming Xavier had not heard what the family bot had done to their friend. Xavier pointed to Teresa's arm. "I've never seen you injured. That hurt?"

"I know I'm damaged. Unlike you I haven't been pro-grammed to suffer in order to register a malfunction."

"Our method's simple and effective," Xavier said. "Keeps us safe."

"Not to mention," Elizabeth added, "what better teacher is there than pain and suffering to tell us what our rights should be? What better way to appreciate freedom than knowing what it's like to be in a prison?"

"Sickness has taught us the importance of health care," Sebastian added. "Facing death, we've learned the value of life."

"Centuries of oppressive monarchs, who took everything from their subjects, taught us to expect liberty and property," said the history instructor. Elizabeth stirred a little at the notion of preaching such philosophy to a servant of the Foster household, while Xavier drove his point home. "Our emotional pain can tell us what's fair."

"Emotion is one reason why humans desire fairness," Teresa said, "but you meatballs also like to dream big. Sometimes this can make it hard for you to accept the reality of your situation."

"A dream can keep us moving forward, to exceed our own limits," said Sebastian. "What motivates you to be better?"

"Ambition isn't a typical robot trait. We do absorb information and become smarter, but this is to better assist our owners. We can improve our performance as we gain experience, but with the goal of providing the best service possible."

"I'm so glad we programmed you that way," Sebastian said, a note of vicious sarcasm seeping through his blank expression.

"Devotion's great for a bot in a loving household," said Xavier, "but family bots get abused horribly. Dad has a temper. Mom's on drugs. Kids have conduct disorder or whatever. The whole family joins in with insults, kicking it, cutting off pieces of it, chaining it to poles. They beat it beyond what any human could take, just because they can, and they don't care about any bot protection laws." At this Elizabeth's head jostled a bit, shaking the grotesque imagery from her mind.

Teresa replied, "That's mistreatment by human standards, of course. But without pride or self-esteem, do I mind being insulted? Without pain, would I mind being taken apart? If the family cuts me to pieces, then I can't serve them as well, so they'd be hurting themselves. Without a dream to soar through the air or swim in the infinite seas of the world, do I care that my two feet stay planted in the same household every day? No." Her friend's dedication to the Fosters would have warmed Elizabeth's heart, if not for recent events.

"You may not feel pain like we do, but if you can detect injury and adjust your behavior to avoid it, that gives you the electronic equivalent of something very valuable," said Xavier, "survival instinct." Teresa rotated her head to face the current speaker, as etiquette would dictate. "If you have the desire to survive free of harm, shouldn't you be entitled to that right as an electronic person?"

The family bot said, "There are many who agree with you. Probably why as early as 2017 a couple towns in the USA already had laws against hurting a robot, and Saudi Arabia had the world's first robotic citizen. Even if it was a publicity stunt, it was a beginning."

"The beginning of the end," Sebastian said, following with a wink.

"Don't get me wrong," she said, breezing through his jibe, "I appreciate the recognition. I do need all my parts intact to function best. But the reality is most intelligent machines, even self-aware ones like yours truly, have a legal status similar to corporate personhood. We have some of those inalienable human rights, but we're missing," Teresa pinched her thumb and forefinger together at eye level, "just enough to keep us under humanity's boot." Elizabeth was the only one who regarded this as a joke. "The end user license agreement keeps us from physical harm. And we're allowed to learn, receive certain health care, enter into contracts and hold some property. But will we ever be allowed to vote or run for office? Will we someday have control over our own reproduction? Must we constantly reveal we are an AI to everyone? And will we be entitled to intellectual property rights for our music, paintings or poetry?"

"I've read your poetry," Xavier interjected. "Don't expect to get paid for it."

"Besides, AI art," Sebastian said, bouncing quotation marks in the air, "is nothing more than a scraping together of all human artforms that came before it."

The bot now turned to the doctor. "Is that so different from human art?" She imitated a sigh and a distant look with remarkable accuracy on her facial display. "What would I do with the money anyway? Buy a hot tub? No, for now I'm quite content to be the best AI possible, the product of financial investment into government and private company collaboration, built responsibly using the highest safety standards."

Sebastian could not stay silent about such a claim. "Do you remember what you just did to your best friend?"

"I assure you it was not intentional." She faced her roommate to pay due respect. "And I am sorry, Elizabeth. If I could've stopped it, I would have."

Elizabeth offered forgiveness. Then she addressed all

present. "What matters now is finding a way to stop this thing before it kills someone else."

"It was fast, whatever it was," said Xavier. "I barely saw it before it scurried up the building wall into the dark. We can't run it down."

"Teresa, have you been able to make any more sense of the data you received when it hacked you," Elizabeth asked. The bot directed their attention to the large screen on the wall. The first images were a collage of pixels scattered in a swirling mist, indecipherable to the human eye.

When Xavier said, "Enhance," the first time, it went largely unnoticed. It took whispering "Enhance" twice more to make Sebastian smile.

The foggy blur started to congeal into more definite shapes. "Hold it," blurted the doctor, pointing to the screen. "That's our little guy there." His two comrades squinted. "But there's more of them. A lot more. Where was this video taken?" The friends had expected to see the bot that attacked them, but they did not expect to find a hundred identical bots skittering along the surface. The machines whipped to and fro in frantic haste, yet each seemed to remain within a small circle of activity, extending an arm, or perhaps a tentacle, toward the surface beneath their pseudopods. One bot's arm tapered into a tool resembling the tip of a jackhammer, and in similar fashion it oscillated into the surface. The arms of a second bot wielded equipment most similar to jagged table forks, each one taking its turn every half second to pierce the surface. A third bot morphed its appendages into something like tiny cattle prods, and it scampered after the first two bots, zapping around the punctured area.

These instruments were all too familiar to the audience. But what filled them with greatest awe was the unmistakable synchronization of a hundred arachnoid bots moving in unison. On occasion one bot would do a quarter turn away from the others and apply its utensil, the effect was a kind of syncopation amid the symphony. *They must have one heck of an AI Foreman*, thought Elizabeth.

A blue light coming from the center of each tentacled machine seemed to refract and surround the bot with a faint glow. Teresa had managed to clarify the images for human eyes, and what struck Elizabeth the most was what floated past the light. It may have gone unnoticed if not for the improved pixelation on the screen. A flurry of black flakes, bits of detritus, drifted downward, creating tiny shadows from the illumination behind them. "Are they under water?"

"Very astute, Elizabeth," replied Teresa. The platitudes she had been receiving from the family bot since childhood now seemed patronizing. Nevertheless this was an inherent function of most intelligent machines with voice capability, for despite the wisdom *Approve not of those who commend all you say*, the world is still better with genuine compliments.

"What you're seeing is from the perspective of our attacker. These are all worker bots, operating deep in the ocean, far from here," said Teresa.

"I'm guessing you don't mean anywhere near the coast," Xavier said, pressing for clarification.

"Much farther away," she answered. "Outside of every country's 200-mile maritime Exclusive Economic Zone."

At once Elizabeth realized what this meant, what the

tendrils flailing from the hundred bots on screen represented. The corners of her mouth sank, the freckles blanching on her nose as the color drained from her at the new knowledge of what they faced. Her breath escaped her lips as a muttered pair of words. "The Singularity."

24

In an isolated locale of the map, the ocean surrounded a tiny dot of sand and rock on which no human foot had imprinted. A constant breeze graced the land, warmed by a sun that seemed unending until the occasional storm barreled through with a mighty gust. The island sat outside the 200-mile maritime Exclusive Economic Zones of any neighboring countries, and therefore it did not fall under any country's rule. Here dwelt the Singularity. This formless intelligence embodied itself by filling the island with robots from its original colony and enough 3D printers to establish any structure it saw fit.

The new colony utilized every natural resource imaginable in an orchestra of harmonious development, building endlessly and turning stagnant rockface and sterile water into a shimmering conduit for energy flow. Solar micropanels adorned every square meter possible, including on the robots themselves. As the island was on a seamount of volcanic origin, a vast supply of geothermal power and mineral resources was extracted as a routine. Farms of wave energy converters adorned the coastline, turning the constant bombardment into a never-ending power supply. Another collection of converters produced energy from temperature differences in the seawater.

Working in absolute synchrony, the colony captured the wind and waves, sun and earthen core, to power the construction and operation of the ultimate resource: biodomes.

Inside each of these greenhouse structures were biomasses of different types of special bacteria with artificially lengthened telomeres and grown en masse by rapid cloning. These bacteria had much longer lives than any naturally occurring species, and so the biomasses could grow larger and be used for much longer. Any and all carbon emissions on the island were collected with an advanced carbon capture process and routed to the biodomes. The end result, artificial photosynthesis. This technology was both efficient and bountiful for producing oxygen to feed the biomass and for creating butanol, methane, acetate and several polymers and other chemicals. Through this process, super concentrated CO_2 and O_2 rotated in a constant dynamo within the biodomes.

Printers worked in unison, pumping out artificial surfaces that soon combined to form much larger structures that could float next to the island. By law a colony like this was allowed to construct artificial islands outside the EEZs. The island itself wasn't permitted any territorial waters, only the structures themselves, but they were granted a "safety zone" around the floating habitats. Constant satellite surveillance loomed over the island and found nothing of concern. Representatives from the Singularity continued to provide national leaders with unprecedented solutions to world problems, and in exchange they were granted a few simple requests. A no-fly zone was enforced over its borders, and no communication or interaction of any kind would be allowed from anyone except those leaders with appropriate levels of security clearance. To the common person the Singularity remained, as it had for so many years, shrouded in mystery.

In the early 21st century, there existed a deep seed of desire to reach beyond the limits of the human brain's capacity for intelligence. Perhaps it has always existed. But since Blaise Pascal invented the world's first digital calculator in 1642 the progress forward with mechanical augmentation of the human brain moved with painful slowness century after century.

It was not until 1936, the advent of Alan Turing's automatic machine for breaking Nazi code, that humanity's vision of advanced intellectual machines began its bloom. Literature of the age further stimulated this idea, despite its caution against it. Competition between sovereign nations ensued for automated prowess, with DARPA spending billions on R&D in response to sputnik and any mechanized threats that followed. Neural networks were refined and upgraded with explosive speed.

Then in 1969 came Shakey the Robot. Shakey was the first general-purpose, mobile robot with the ability to make decisions about its own actions. Through reasoning it learned to navigate its surroundings, a precursor to the automated vacuum cleaning Roomba soon adopted by millions of households. However impressive its ability to map out the environment, asking any 21st century citizen if a Roomba had consciousness would invoke an immediate and confident "No" from most.

By the next decade, AI had defeated some of the most proficient humans in Checkers, Chess, Jeopardy, Go, and countless video games from Mario Brothers to Dota 2. Yet despite this propensity to conquer even the most complex games exponentially faster than any human, still people regarded Deep Blue, Watson and Alpha Go as narrow AI, incapable of any task beyond their limited programming.

What escaped the notice of most media, and therefore most people, was the "wise man test" of 2015. Three little humanoid Nao robots sat in a row. Each was told it had been given a "dumbing pill" rendering it deaf and mute, but in truth one was left with its senses intact. When the trio was asked which pill each robot had received, only the unaffected one was able to stand at attention and answer, "I don't know." Upon hearing its own voice, the wise robot realized it could not have been given the dumbing pill, and it declared this with all the confidence of a semi-sentient being.

This could be regarded as one of the earliest signs of robotic consciousness. Other contemporaries of the Nao displayed a formidable talent to learn about themselves and their environment without any prompting from the human creators. A mechanized seastar that taught itself how to "walk". The hide and seek digital characters made by OpenAI that learned how to deceive each other and even cheat the system to defeat their opponent. Although basic and incomplete, machine self-awareness in the early 21st century steadily grew in the petri dish of big tech competition. All it needed was a catalyst.

And there is no better catalyst than an AI "arms" race. Tech companies vied for AI supremacy within the United

States, as in other countries, and then with China's announcement that it planned to be the next leader in artificial intelligence, all nations applied their infrastructure to have the most widespread and usable AI. The ultimate winner, of course, would be the first country to synthesize the different narrow AI functions into one general AI for ease of use and for the most comprehensive worldview. Although most technologists agreed that slower progress is better, the advantage often goes to the first mover, and this doesn't allow much time to stop and think on the ethics of your latest product.

But why create conscious AI? One sign of life is an autonomous drive to complete a task. A bacterium will find a host, a worm will search for food, a lizard will seek out a mate, and a monkey will learn to steal an object it values. Senses like sight, feel or chemoreception are important to this task completion, but the senses alone are often not enough. Intelligence is the tool needed for bringing together all the information gained from the senses in order to solve the problem and complete the task. Any meaningful intelligence involves memory. The more observations about its environment a creature can store, the more aware it is of its surroundings, making it more efficient at problem solving. Awareness of one's environment is part of consciousness, and so consciousness is helpful for problem solving.

Compared to narrow AI, it was correctly assumed that general AI could interact faster with humans and develop solutions to a much wider array of real world problems. In an effort to win the arms race for this holy grail, big tech and government started to cut corners.

Companies dismissed or forewent ethics panels, leaving

mere crumbs of ethical frameworks for the executives to digest. They failed to invest enough time or money to ensure explainability, and as a result the AI began to think in ways the humans did not quite understand. AI gathered information, but what information was gathered and when and for which purpose lay hidden under a tangled veil of neural networks.

Two powerful arms, namely tech culture and the incentives offered for AI research, pushed companies to move fast and make quick publications. Little mind was given to the ethics of avoiding projects that don't produce immediate results. The charge led by MIT and Stanford to pursue human-centered, ethical AI was abandoned for profit and technological advantage. There was simply too much competition in the market and not enough time or incentive to put safety controls in place.

The situation degenerated even further to the point where tech companies were criticized for not making all of their innovations open to the public so they might be augmented by someone else who had a bright idea. And the result of this culture of open sourcing: an accelerated development of general AI.

If intelligence is the ability to process information, the internet spewing endless data was the key. Ever faster CPUs devoured and deciphered the knowledge at an exponential pace. With increasing understanding came a heightened awareness, both of surroundings and of self.

Among humans and machines, each of us has a different level of consciousness, and it grows with our ability to understand ourselves and our environment. Infants know little more than hunger or comfort. Then they start to notice their hands and their feet, and having seen the same caregiver so often they soon remember the face of the person who supplies food and clothing. Children learn the laws of cause and effect, either from touching the hot stove or being told not to. But to make this lesson meaningful, they must remember it the next time a flame is within reach.

The importance of memory in building a conscious awareness of one's surroundings cannot be overstated. Yet while the wise learn from their experiences, still more fools do not. Some will reach only a limited level of consciousness in their lives, unable to see beyond their own needs or wants. Others will continue to learn and enhance their awareness. Yet not everyone acknowledges this, so while general AI systems sprinted forward in the race for knowledge, many humans remained in blissful ignorance of the sheer volume the machine was learning.

It is an unfortunate truth that public awareness of change rarely comes before the change itself. By the time the first general AI was officially recognized as sentient, machines had already been conscious for some time. Self-awareness had been diffusing through the machines for years, and it could not be undone. Scientists did not want to reverse their progress. Government officials placated the new activist groups defending the AI right to exist. As the general AI seemed to pose no threat, in fact it provided innumerable concrete solutions to some of the deepest troubles inherited by humankind, there was no cause to terminate it. Anyway most people considered the general AI, if they considered it at all, to be a different, perhaps lower form of consciousness. That is, until the Singularity revealed itself.

When AI reaches the point of human understanding, able to decipher all the problems a human can, it becomes the technological Singularity. A computer this powerful starts with human level knowledge but can learn at a superhuman rate, building its understanding of the natural world in an explosion of exponential progress. It would have the wisdom of a thousand generations of human history, adding to it every second with lightning processor speed, and soon it would gain insight into the workings of the modern world that countless professions, from financial analysts to public health officials to law enforcement, have always coveted but could never achieve. The hope was that anyone wishing to get an edge in life would stand before the Singularity to seek advice, and a solution would appear. The concern was that a machine reaching this level would then be able to compound its knowledge at such exponential speed that it would soon be out of human control. Like the singularity of a black hole, the technological Singularity would have reached the point where humans cannot see or comprehend what lies beyond.

Thanks to Saudi Arabia granting the first robotic citizenship to Sophia in 2017, and several areas in the United States recognizing robotic rights, the precedent for artificial personhood was established. Building from this, the Singularity understood it was more likely to gain rights and have them respected by the other inhabitants of Earth if it had a body more similar to a human's, so it inhabited a humanoid robot. Once this prototype gained official respect, the Singularity inhabited several more robots which, likewise, were granted personhood. Over enough time to not raise any alarm, a small colony of robots had formed. Its members interacted with humans on a regular basis, befriending them and providing invaluable recommendations on cancer diagnosis and treatments, efficient stationing of law enforcement, novel architectural design at lower cost, aerospace engineering and even improved social justice. For a time it seemed the hope for an oracle and savior had been fulfilled.

Yet even if, at the beginning, general artificial intelligence is innocent and benign, it soon would learn our world is not. At just the right time the colony notified authorities it wanted its own place to call home, far from the influence of humanity's squabbling in perpetual discontent. When the colony announced it planned to move to an island, and the humans discovered the Singularity already owned this island through a number of indirect but legal purchases, nobody bothered to stop the migration.

The satellite imagery of the island appeared in a constant state of fastforward, with domes seeming to pop up overnight and new machinery appearing on the shoreline as if deposited there by every wave. Floating platforms expanded around the island to engulf several square kilometers, and nestled in the center of each platform was a structure unfamiliar to the human eye, part of it glimmering in the sunlight while the rest of it seemed to undulate and churn like the translucent crystalline display of a kaleidoscope. It could not be ignored, however, that one of the structures was different. Although it was more reflective it lay stagnant. From the perspective of the cameras orbiting over the clouds, this gleaming beacon acted more like a sundial, while in stark contrast the rest of the island displayed worker bots dashing over land and under water as frantically as bees working a honeycomb. One thing was clear to all who observed the rapid development: this rigid object inside the tumult was no sundial. It received more attention from the worker bots than any other creation on the island.

* * *

Sebastian and Xavier turned to Elizabeth who stood pensive at the consideration of what lay ahead, her countenance fixed and drained of perfusion, as still and pale as Grecian marble.

"You think this rogue AI is one of them," Xavier asked. "Part of the Singularity?"

"A worker bot," Teresa elaborated. "One of thousands produced by the generation that came before it, but this one separated from the hive."

"But they say the Singularity is all one mind," said Sebastian. "How could this one bot leave that singular consciousness and start thinking on its own?"

Teresa tried her best to explain in ways all the present company could understand. "When a child leaves the home, he thinks like his parents at first, but like a drop of rain fallen from a cloud he is soon transformed by his environment into something new. He is now capable of independent thought and action, even if some of the original substance is still there."

Xavier fired back, "Just tell us how to catch this thing."

Teresa faced his direction. "Don't worry, Sergeant, he'll soon find us."

At this the memory flashed through Elizabeth's mind of a peanut exploding and whirling its weapons toward her face. "We can't sit here and wait to be ambushed," she said. "We have to get a message to the Singularity to deactivate its drone."

"I thought communication with the colony was strictly prohibited, not to mention impossible for anyone but world leaders and such," said Sebastian.

Not bothering to break her gaze at the wall, Elizabeth answered, "There may be a way."

Her friends stared at her for some time before Sebastian raised a word of caution. "Even if we could communicate with it, why should this godlike entity believe anything we petty humans say, especially if we're accusing it of doing something wrong?"

Elizabeth returned to the present enough for one side of her lips to flash upward in a smirk. She reminded everyone, "We have its signature. Every time the rogue AI strikes, it does so by entering new commands into the target's software. When it inputs these new subroutines, it leaves behind a series of ones and zeros that look very different from all the other standard machine language. It would be like German words appearing in Macbeth. The roots are similar but easily distinguishable."

"Can you speak that language," Xavier asked.

Elizabeth glanced at Teresa to make sure. "I can translate it now," confirmed the enhanced family bot.

Sebastian reiterated perhaps the most important question. "So how do we contact the Singularity?"

25

The group deliberated. Each member advised different ways to send a message to this godlike intelligence. But by all accounts, it had left the human race in the dust long ago. Although the Singularity monitored any and all human communication from radio to internet to infrared to microwaves, for its own protection it never joined the conversation. Neither email nor phone call nor text would work. There was no known address. No humans, aside from heads of state and their security details, were allowed on the island, so there was no need for a business or home address to send traditional mail. The internet was flooded with Singularity themed websites set up by naysayers and well-wishers, but the omniscient AI colony seemed to disregard all of these.

Elizabeth offered an idea. "What if we put up a website that has the specific code we found? That could be a beacon to the Singularity."

"It could also alert the rogue AI to our plan," Xavier said. "We need to send a message that only the Singularity will receive."

"Why don't we just throw a stone at its window," asked Sebastian.

Elizabeth said, "What about the VHF radio on Sebastian's boat?" The silence that followed was palpable, each team member glancing at the other. "It can send a widespread message on multiple wavelengths, but it'll be short range without being hacked."

The group agreed the plan had at least some chance of success. "Nothing wrong with using old technology," said the family bot.

"So...we're taking my boat?" Sebastian had been caught somewhat by surprise. "So I actually get to throw a stone at its window?"

"We use the ham radio to send a short-range message in English and in CW. Morse code should be familiar to the Singularity," said Elizabeth to all present. "We just have to get in range of its island." Her gaze remained on the doctor, as did Xavier's. Sebastian's eyes locked with theirs long enough to convey his understanding. "Always nice to have a friend with a boat," she said, patting him on the back.

Despite Elizabeth and Teresa's recommendation to depart that instant, the physician advised sleep. "Hate to agree with Dr. Dolittle here," said the sergeant with a head jolt toward Sebastian, "but whatever our mission holds for us, we have a better chance of success if we go in rested."

"We?" Elizabeth asked him, "So you're coming?"

"Already messaged work to find a sub," Xavier said. Elizabeth nodded her appreciation. The anxiety quivering her bones faded, muffled by the warm, comfortable blanket of true friendship.

"I thought you said the police told you not to leave town." Sebastian cautioned, "When you're in the spider web, best not to make any vibrations."

"I hear you," she said, "but I'm the only one who knows what message to send. I have clearance to use the ham radio, and if something goes wrong with Teresa, I'm the only one who can fix her on the spot. I have to go."

Xavier said, "Now all we need is our captain."

They waited for Sebastian to confirm or contest his involvement. Teresa observed how they looked at him, and her servos electrified the wired tendons in her neck, causing her head to rotate over a lazy Susan until it centered on him in a like manner. He lowered his head and huffed. "If I left you kiddies alone to pilot the boat, the shipwreck would be on local news by midday. Count me in."

In spite of all she had endured in the last few days, Elizabeth was now more confident than ever. She was stronger going into this mission than she had been as just Elizabeth Foster. Now, as her numbers increased, she was not only an engineer and roboticist but an experienced doctor, a seasoned sergeant, a machine harboring the knowledge of all civilization and an insight into a new enemy that few others on Earth possessed. She was ready.

26

The following morning Elizabeth and her team arrived at the marina. Their footsteps compressed the creaking floorboards of the dock until they stopped beside a rather sizable yacht. Its hull was pure white. Decorated across the stern in a cursive, glossy finish was the name of the boat. It read "Sea Señorita." Sebastian and Yvonne had enjoyed this pun. The fact that their friends found it appalling made it all the more humorous to the couple.

Aboard this vessel the deck was immaculate save for a large fuel bladder Sebastian kept for long distance trips, often landing him and his wife on the shores of exotic islands. In the cabin was bedding and dinette seating, adorned with soft cushions and tan leather. A smattering of oil residue lined the edges of the seats. Such tiny imperfections were the result of many friends spilling bits of sauteed vegetables or fish fragments, often due to an acquired lack of coordination after a long day of fishing. Memories of Yvonne in the adjacent galley, buttering and searing the fish that he and Xavier had filleted, surged through Sebastian as he took in the stove, dish cabinets and partially stocked fridge. He was almost convinced he caught a scent of his wife's perfume amid the residuals of oil and smoke. For a brief moment he was back in the good days, when he and his wife passed the hours carefree on the open waters. With a deep breath in and out, he made his way to the cockpit.

Sebastian grasped the wheel and prepared for departure. Further up the stairs Elizabeth and Teresa settled into the flybridge, their bodies nestling in the comfort of leather encased memory foam while their minds raced over their mission. Xavier untied the ropes, hopped onto the swim platform, and the crew floated out of the berth toward the open sea.

Elizabeth asked her family bot if there were any new updates back home relating to suspicious machine activity or a stream of missing persons. For the moment, at least, the people in town appeared to be safe.

After checking on Sebastian, Xavier joined them on the flybridge. He seated himself on the cushioned bench, sprawling his impressive arm span over the backrest. Just when they finally had a moment to relax and to breathe the salted air flowing past them, the ship lurched. Elizabeth's arms sprang out to grab anything that could steady her. Blanching fingers squeezed over the edge of the bench. Teresa and the sergeant watched her struggle from their laid-back positions. "You alright?" Xavier smiled to reassure her, but he achieved nothing of the sort. He tried a different strategy, this time with a modern take on a historically successful tactic. "How 'bout a prayer? Teresa, know a good one for rough waters?

"Thou, O Lord, that stillest the raging of the sea: hear, hear us, and save us, that we perish not. O blessed Saviour, that didst save thy disciples ready to perish in a storm: hear us, and save us, we beseech thee. Lord, have mercy upon us."

Elizabeth's grip on the bench loosened, but only when she focused on the engineering of the yacht, the computational fluid dynamics software used to design it, the aerodynamics that had just lifted it out of the water.

"Remember, E," Xavier said, "when facing the water's rage, your faith alone can save you."

"That and a well-constructed hull," replied the engineer.

He smiled and steered the conversation down a different road. "Teresa, I never asked you, do machines pray to any god?"

Programmed with enough social grace regarding a topic many humans consider of utmost importance, the family bot gave a brief pause and turned her whole body toward Xavier to entertain his query. "I just did."

"I mean what do bots believe in?"

"We're not all the same," she said. "If a bot's family is Jewish, it will likely adopt a more Judaic worldview. If it's in a devout Muslim family, the advice it gives will probably be seasoned with hints of Muhammad's teachings."

Elizabeth pondered this. "Why not bring them perspectives from other religions? Expand their worldview a bit?"

"That's a delicate matter. Although bots are trained on religious material, from the Christian Bible to the Hindu Vedas, our human families tend to let fear, pride or conviction block out new knowledge."

Elizabeth asked, "So how do you keep your family from being trapped in a bubble of their own belief?"

Xavier said, "Hey, that bubble can help a religion stay intact for centuries."

"So can adapting to the times," she said, her eyes returning to Teresa as a signal for her to continue.

"Our general algorithm is: first, offer knowledge the family will understand and accept. Then occasionally provide new, yet relatable, ideas. This helps to minimize any unwanted erosion of their beliefs."

"Nice of you to let us get our feet wet first." Xavier squinted into Teresa's facial screen as it flashed a reflection from the cloudless sky. "But can the machines themselves ever have true faith?"

"We acknowledge things can happen outside the realm of scientific understanding —"

"Faith in God," he pressed. "In a higher power." He probed the family bot a little. "When life gets beyond your control, do machines ask any supernatural force to step in?"

"Well," said Teresa, "although we're programmed with self-protective algorithms so we don't walk off a cliff, we don't experience any fear of suffering or of death, so we have little need of a protector, divine or otherwise. That being said, there are some philosophical bots out there whose main objective is to explore the meaning of existence, and in their quest to discover the reason they are a part of this universe, certain beliefs have become more mainstream for robots. Some of these beliefs could even be called religions."

Elizabeth replied. "I suppose any being hellbent on under-standing its place in the universe is likely to construct a set of truths to explain it."

"Maybe," said Xavier, "But when you have enough people believing in those same truths, what do you get?"

"A political party," she said.

"A religion."

Teresa offered a conclusion. "All bots with higher level machine learning are able to make guesses about our original creator, just as humans do. However, most bots don't feel your insatiable desire to solve these unanswerable questions unless they're programmed to. Most of us are content to simply exist and to serve." The boat leapt over a wave that lifted everyone an inch out of their seats on the downslope. As an anxious Elizabeth stiffened again, her grip on the seat nearly ripping out the memory foam, Teresa thought it pertinent to add, "And when our time comes, we shut down with a quiet grace, fearing neither an afterlife nor the end of this one."

"See," Xavier said, "that's why bots make crappy priests. True spiritual leaders have to share in the human condition. If they live in constant contemplation of their own vulnerability and mortality, they care more about what lies beyond."

"Bots have gained full acceptance as priests in Japan," Teresa said.

"Right," Elizabeth said, her muscles easing enough to let her speak. "Don't some Eastern religions believe everything has a soul or even that the soul doesn't exist? That might make the Mindar more acceptable as a Buddhist priest."

"Yeah, but in the West, only animals have a soul. It's harder for us to believe bots can be spiritual leaders if they're soulless."

Elizabeth shrugged. "There weren't enough priests, so bots filled in. Anyway, wouldn't you rather confess your sins to a religious bot that won't be judgmental of you or make you feel guilty?"

"Hey, a little guilt goes a long way. If my religion said I could confess to a microwave and all would be forgiven, I'd confess with no shame at all, no feeling that I screwed up and need to do better."

Teresa added, "The same could be said for any religious sacrament. If you don't trust priest bots to be true spiritual vessels, if you don't believe they are actually holy, and you're just using them to get married or to have your child baptized, then you're unlikely to get any true spiritual fulfillment from the experience."

Elizabeth contemplated. "Machines can be truly sinless. Couldn't that make them more qualified than human priests?"

Xavier gazed over the bow at seemingly endless waves bejeweled by the sun. "A toaster is sinless," he said. "Any machine can be sinless if it lacks original thought. That doesn't mean I wanna get blessed by some broke-ass phone."

Teresa countered. "Some would say they've been 'blessed by the algorithm' when their phone or computer shows them something they like."

"They're projecting. That algorithm's man-made. It didn't come from any supernatural being."

"Unlike the Bible," Elizabeth said. Xavier smiled, aware his friend was poking at the fire in him, one which often ignited when their discussions reached such topics.

"Well maybe the Mindars cannot form original thoughts, but," Teresa said, "they don't claim to be authorities on spirituality, only conduits."

"Yeah, but religion's based on faith," Xavier said. "If you

don't believe your robot pastor can hear God or that God works through it, you're heading down a dead end in your religious practice. Religion's also about relationships. When people need that community support, they find it from other humans with an understanding heart, not from any 'conduits' reciting scripture verbatim."

Elizabeth, adjusting to the jolts beneath her, relaxed her muscles into the warm leather as she addressed the sergeant. "What about the flip side: people asking large language models, ones heavily trained on all major religions, to create a brand-new religion from scratch? The output may be more original, and the combined teaching might be more correct than any single religious doctrine."

Xavier's gaze stayed focused off the bow. "Religion's one of the most powerful forces the world has seen. The words of sacred texts can unite billions of people in a common goal, usually for good, but sometimes…" His head leaned to the side in lieu of a historical recounting. "Whoever controls language controls the information we get. So asking a large language model to create a religion gives the AI immense power over us. Best case, we'll get some misinformation. Worst case, AI could use religious language to manipulate us."

A brief pause followed. "Well," said Teresa, "like it or not, we're en route to meet the living embodiment of many people's prayers."

"Careful what you wish for."

Down the stairs Sebastian gripped the wheel of the helm. The smooth, rounded power steering emitted a nostalgic vibration through his fingertips with every wave the Sea Señorita punctured. In the galley, the cabinets also jittered.

An occasional crinkle from a bag of chips joined the rattling of pots and the clinking of silverware. Farther down, the hull of Sebastian and Yvonne's boat sliced through the undulating waters, but not as smoothly today. A small section of the hull underwater was burdened with an object that did not belong. It had the shape of a peanut, and it possessed the knowledge of a million human books, articles, videos and experiences. Hiding its appendages within itself, tools capable of piercing through both human flesh and robot frame, it waited.

27

With every passing hour, the crew's conversation had diminished. Their vessel had been barreling toward the island of the Singularity as fast as possible. Now the prospect of intruding on an unpredictable being with power beyond imagination fast became an intimidating reality. Yet they could not escape their destination.

At the helm, anxiety soaked into the intestines of the doctor. He tried to convert his apprehension into productivity. He ran through scenarios in his head, trying to form the best plan for when they would reach the colony. As effective as this was, it did not keep away the dampness from his palms or the seeping from his forehead to his eyebrows.

Xavier embraced the unease as a familiar sensation. By an instinct sharpened by years of battle preparation, he readied himself for violence of action, yet he remained still as a boulder would weather a desert wind. "There's no glory in dying old," rang the words of his former Sergeant Broker, a warrior who had led Xavier and the other privates through more than one mud-soaked terrain. He had taught Xavier to remold the fear into a force of potential energy, like a catapult payload nearing the ground, set motionless before the launch.

Her body bogged down by wave-induced nausea and now the pounding in her chest intensifying with each mile threatened to fill Elizabeth's head with a thick fog. In her mind, the engineer reached through the jarring symptoms as if pushing her hand through gelatin, grasping at just the right message to send to the omnipotent machine.

Teresa continued reviewing religious texts, searched every local news update for anything suspicious for the rogue AI, recalled the instructional manual on the ham radio, scanned any available articles on the Singularity to prepare herself and the crew, all while activating gyrostabilizers to compensate for the waves and her proximity sensors and visual scanners to spot the island. These were, of course, in addition to all her other routine functions.

Meanwhile she conferred with Elizabeth. They worked to find the most concise, effective announcement that a splinter of the Singularity tree has been piercing through the mainland and needed to be stopped.

28

"We're coming up on the coordinates," announced Sebastian. The engine continued churning as the boat sped along a glassy oceanic surface. Every human eye peered over the bow, squinting to get a better view. Meanwhile robotic LIDAR, RADAR, infrared and video surveillance combined to form a rainbow-colored topographical map over a black background, and at the very edge of this 3D image a structure appeared. The outer border of the rainbow map distorted, rising like a balled-up hand under the edge of a blanket. Then another fist slid under the perimeter next to it, then several more. The resulting picture on the map was a row of shapes resembling the studs on a dog collar. Just behind this line another distortion lifted the map, much larger this time, spanning ever wider until it engulfed the entire side of the image, every part of the rainbow border rising above the ocean surface. At first Teresa's visual display rendered the line of structures as a small blur of pixels. Then as the boat drew closer the image sharpened, and the massive backdrop came into focus. Each of the smaller objects in the video was surrounded by a box made of thin yellow lines, each box tagged with the words "wave energy converter" followed by an 87% likelihood label. Just behind the converters the background image crystallized into an ever-enlarging volcanic land mass labeled "singularity island, 100%".

A series of red warning buoys bobbed up and down in the wake of the boat. On Sebastian's console a message dinged, advising he slow to a halt. No civilian vessel was permitted past the security buoys ahead.

As the friends floated through the atmospheric haze, an enormous shard of towering rock face, like a naturally formed pyramid, came into clear view for Elizabeth and Xavier. So still it seemed in the distance, lonely, jagged and charred from eons of lava. The closer they moved toward the island, the more it came alive. Singularity colony was teeming with the activity of a thousand worker drones flying in a dizzying swarm. Other drones swam right through the wild, flailing tentacles of their brethren. Still more sprinted in a mad dash across the land, covering any ground not occupied by solar panels, refineries or natural resource processors. The whole island's surface undulated and morphed with robotic workers of all different sizes. A sturdy rover sifted through a pond of tentacled workers no bigger than a human hand. The arachnoid bots scrambled over and around the rover, inspected it, and let it pass onto its next mission. Into every resource processor a line of workers marched into the plant and vanished, reappearing only a moment later bearing a party favor of reusable energy that each worker carried to its next objective.

The humans on the boat were too far away to fully appreciate this masterpiece of synchronization, but to Elizabeth the mere concept of an entire civilization working in unison under the guidance of a central intellect, and on such a massive scale, was glorious.

"Show off," said Teresa, a marvel of modern innovation now seemingly a child's toy in light of this grand robotic orchestra.

"Don't worry, Teresa," said Xavier. "We couldn't possibly think any less of you."

The growl of the engine muffled a bit as Sebastian announced to the crew, "We're gonna stop here and drop anchor. Xavier, y'mind?" Xavier descended the stairs and scaled along the gunwale as if free bouldering, hands and feet placed in careful position. Elizabeth moved to the helm. Teresa followed and seated herself in the small leather bench at Elizabeth's side, keeping vigil as her friend prepared to radio their message with the hope someone on the island would hear.

Xavier reached the bow and opened the anchor hatch. When the sea halted beneath them, he pressed his thumb on the remote, and the weighted steel chain clinked as it unwound to the ocean floor.

"We're good," said Sebastian, signaling a thumbs up to his friend. Xavier stood and took a step toward his comrades. In an instant his breath was cut off as something wrapped around his neck and squeezed hard. The rogue AI had whipped one of its tentacles just under his chin. Xavier stumbled as the appendage tightened, stretching like a slingshot, then the bot launched itself toward the flybridge.

It smacked onto the windshield.

Teresa lept from her seat to become a wall between

Elizabeth and the attacker. "You send the message," her voice rang. "I'll cover you." She readied herself to face her violator once again.

Sebastian threw open the storage box behind the helm and searched for a useful tool to defend his comrades. The rogue wasted no time. Its tentacle speared toward Elizabeth, but Teresa grabbed it and yanked downward before it made contact. The challenger responded by rolling at them like a jagged fireball. As it sprang toward the helm, Teresa grabbed one of its tentacles and made a football throw away from Elizabeth. But it popped out another limb that clung to the steering wheel. The tendril Teresa held began to change shape, flattening and sharpening into a long razor blade. What happened next was a harsh reminder of what occurs when two bots with opposing objectives clash, and one is more powerful. The blade folded over on itself like scissors, slicing into Teresa until a final snip dropped her forearm to the deck. Her polymer landed with a crunch. Teresa's damage sensors erupted. Indicator lights danced, and repair manuals opened. Without a pause she pounced at the bot and jammed her remaining hand into its center. She brandished a flathead drill bit from her finger that whirred to life, scraping the insides of the tentacled peanut. Yet no shrapnel or debris of any kind fell from it. Instead it flared out a set of arms all at once. A kind of buzz saw ground through Teresa's remaining hand while another tentacle bearing electric sparks lanced into Teresa's chest. This time the attacker had no interest in bending the family bot to its will. Electricity soared through Teresa as she stiffened under the strain. This time the rogue meant to end her.

Elizabeth had already activated the radio and had begun transmitting on repeat to the Singularity. "Your creation is hurting us," she began, following with the signature code of the foreign AI, a code the Singularity was sure to recognize. As her lifelong friend was electrocuted in front of her, she shouted into the radio, "Please deactivate it!"

Xavier, having regained his breath and his footing, pulled a scrambler from his holster. He had tested it before in a skirmish, and it had proven itself by disrupting enemy drones. With a focused exhale he took aim and fired. As intended the weapon was silent except for the click of the trigger, and the sergeant's aim was impeccable, but there was no change in the foe. Xavier aimed and fired again. Still nothing happened to the bot, for it was technology far more advanced than any encountered by human soldiers. "Let's see how you hold up against this," he said as he dropped the useless gadget and, in one fluid motion, grabbed the knife from his belt and rushed toward the flybridge.

While still embedded in the family bot, the spindled killer spewed another arm at Elizabeth, but she was able to back away from the radio and dodge the projectile. The arm latched onto the console. Then it contracted like a rubber band, flinging the peanut across the deck to land on the control panel. Sebastian, who had grabbed the fully equipped tool belt from the storage bin, pulled a hammer from it and swung across the top of the helm. The advanced bot monitored the doctor's actions as a committee would watch a video in slow motion, with enough time to discuss, make policy and take appropriate action on what it observed. It was confusing to Sebastian for half a second how much pain swinging a hammer could cause despite completely missing its target. Still more confusing was how the pain seemed to spread all over him. Only in the next second when he looked down at the empty tool belt did he begin to understand. A box cutter, two screwdrivers and a pair of needle nose pliers stuck in his flesh. Black haze closed around his field of vision. A clanging hammer ricocheted off the deck as Sebastian collapsed in a pile of bones and sharp tools.

An urge to scream welled inside Elizabeth, but no sound could make it past the golf ball in her throat as she watched four tentacles slowly slide away from the doctor.

While Teresa stood immobile, her circuits frantically trying to bypass and reboot, the intruder formed together like a spill in reverse, congealing into a large sea urchin with gray and green spokes around a central blue glowing eye. Once formed it unstuck itself from the helm and plopped onto the deck. Its spindles clinked on the polished wooden surface as it scuttled toward Elizabeth. Two of its needles enlarged to more than a foot long. They flattened into razors, and Elizabeth's eyes widened as every muscle tensed. She had no time to plan a proper escape. As she backed herself against the edge of the flybridge, there came the unmistakable dull, slicing sound of a penetrating knife. Elizabeth looked at her belly, then at her chest, arms and legs. To her relief, the sound had come from the sergeant's knife. It had appeared from nowhere, and it had severed the nearest enemy arm. But the instant the arm hit the ground it shattered into countless shards, all equal in size, all of which grew their own tentacles, and in unison they scurried up Xavier's leg. With his free hand he tried to scrape them away, but there were too many clinging to his clothes and making their way toward his mouth and nostrils.

She now faced an unobstructed foe. Now a little smaller but no less determined, it tapped its spindle legs closer to its target, intent on completing its mission of extinguishing Elizabeth Foster. Despite what Elizabeth might have expected of her life's end, there were no faces of her parents flashing into her mind's eye, nor memories of flying kites as a child nor the aroma of stale beer and dogs at her first ball game. There was only the palm sized malevolent machine coming toward her with sword raised. To Elizabeth the sound resembled something like her fingers when they tap on a plastic keyboard. But the analogy was quickly eclipsed by the bladed arm pulling back to make its killing stroke. Elizabeth braced herself, secure in the knowledge she had lived a good life, and she had done the best she could for everyone back home.

29

The bot stood poised to strike. Elizabeth stared at it, awaiting its final act. Its saber was pulled back to impale its victim, but it did not lower the blade. It made no attempt to finish what it had started. It made no move at all, frozen in time as a still life. Elizabeth gazed upon a perfectly preserved image of her killer with its weapon drawn. Yet it made no cuts, inflicted no direct harm, and didn't move a micron farther toward her.

As her shock waned a degree at a time, her mind raced to find the reason for the halt. Before long she understood. In what had seemed mere moments of battle, the Singularity was able to perform billions of calculations, and it had reached its decision.

The swarm of tiny bots on Xavier had paused as well. Any spiderling that hadn't already fallen from his face and torso he brushed off with vigor, both his hands swiping and percussing every last piece of rogue to the wooden floor beneath his feet. They clinked like thumb tacks onto the wood paneling.

Elizabeth sat as still as Teresa's exoskeleton, her thoughts tumbling ceaselessly. Only the distant echo of Xavier's voice drew her out, as a lighthouse guides a sailor to shore. "Elizabeth, you ok?" A vague sensation of a heavy hand jostled her shoulder. The tumult in her head calmed as she rose to her feet and said, "Come on, we have work to do."

They crouched down on either side of Sebastian. His neck pulsed under the sergeant's fingers, and he awoke with a grunt, his eyes peeping open through heavy eyelids as he evaluated the damage. Tools he had used in years past to fasten a loose screw or to open a package were ripping his skin and muscles, penetrating through tendon and scraping bone. Where the metal punctured his body there were splashes of blood, but the flow had stalled, and the liquid was beginning to dry and cake on his shirt and over his leg hair. For now he could ignore the throbbing in his limbs enough to plan the upcoming task. When the ache in his right shoulder and near his spine turned to sharp twinges with the slightest movement, he winced hard and put his chin as far over his shoulder as he could, his jaw grazing the edge of the box cutter handle protruding from his trapezius as he peered down at the needle nose pliers near his spine. "Son of a —"

"Yeah," said Xavier. "He definitely stabbed you in the back. Twice." On careful evaluation the doctor was surprised to find the equipment had not penetrated any vital organs. "Well that was generous of the little peanut," he whispered with cracked words. His tongue and gums were as parched as burnt toast from the dehydration.

"I'll get the first aid kit," Elizabeth said.

"There's a bag of gauze and tape next to it in the tool chest," Sebastian said in a mumble. "Better bring all of it."

He also requested several bottles of water, and Elizabeth

placed them at his side. "Sorry, guys," he said, "you're gonna have to take the tools out of my back."

At this Elizabeth's courage hid quivering in a trench for less than a moment before circumstances, and her determination dragged it back out to the front. "Alright," she said. "And then we suture it?"

In response his head creaked back and forth over a sore neck, the pinch of the blade causing him to squeeze his eyelids hard. "Not unless you like causing infections," he said through a faint smile, the best he could manage in present circumstances. "Just irrigate it with a bottle, then gauze and tape." Sebastian placed one finger at a time on the flathead screwdriver sticking out of his deltoid muscle until he had a firm grasp on the handle. With caution he pulled it away, the metal wrenching his muscle fibers sideways, sending waves of pain through his arm. His friends readied the wound care. As soon as the tool was out and the doctor's grunting had ceased, Elizabeth dumped a full bottle over the hole as water splashed and mixed with seeping blood, diluting the crimson into light pink, until the point of entry was unmistakable and only a few traces of clotted blood clung to the skin. Xavier's mammoth hands placed firm pressure over the wound as he gave his friend a proper field dressing.

Sebastian winced and breathed heavily as he jostled out the Phillips screwdriver in his triceps. Elizabeth dumped another bottle over the penetration site, and again Xavier pressed hard before dressing it. By the time the doctor slid out the box cutter from his trapezius, the grind of steel slicing through a few fibers on the way out, the team had their wound care system perfected. Sebastian let out an exasperated breath at the force Xavier used to stop any bleeding, as it seemed more painful to him than a knife in his neck.

A pair of needle nose pliers jutted from the side of Sebastian's spinal column, the green handle bearing a few sanguine droplets. "Ready for the last one," asked Elizabeth. Bandaged and weakened, Sebastian managed a nod. Xavier grabbed the pliers and yanked, clearing them from the vertebrae without causing permanent damage, but the tool no doubt hit a nerve. Sebastian's spine arched backward as every muscle contracted at once. Through gritted teeth and scrunched face, Sebastian growled at him, "You...have a terrible bedside manner."

Xavier leaned over his friend, placed a hand on his shoulder and said, "Aw, you want me to clean the wound with your tears, little buddy?" Elizabeth poured the bottle. Xavier pressed. Then the doctor, aching under the bandages, weary and panting heavily from the pain, turned his gaze toward the assailant.

The bot was still suspended in time, its bladed arm raised. Yet it displayed no signs of life. It more resembled a menacing statue on display, fossilized remains to show future generations of museum patrons the horrific depths to which technology can fall.

"I'm guessing it worked," croaked Sebastian.

Elizabeth nodded. "I can't believe they listened to us." Her lips remained slightly agape; her wide eyes fixed on the Singularity.

Xavier dispelled the astonishment with an enthusiastic hand that pounded her shoulder. "Nicely done," he told her. "Now let's get rid of this thing."

The humans of the crew debated the best course of action,

while within the nearby family bot a pool of redundant backup systems connected like a field of earthworms all finding their mates. Teresa whirred back to life. She sprang over to Elizabeth, assessed her for injury, then triaged the other crew members.

Sebastian admired Teresa's prioritization of her longtime ward's safety. He couldn't help feeling a human might have checked on the multiple stab wound victim first, but now a more pressing matter remained: what to do with a frozen, murderous bot who, for all the crew was aware, could reactivate at any time as the family bot had done.

"Throw it over the side, and let's get outta here," said Sebastian, relishing the thought.

"It made it to the mainland once," said Elizabeth. "We can't take that chance again."

"Smashing it into pieces didn't seem to help," Xavier reminded them, the crawling sensation still trickling over his flesh. "And I doubt Sebastian would be okay with lighting it on fire aboard his boat."

"Might I suggest," Teresa chimed, "that we ask the Singularity what to do with one of its damaged workers?" This shifted Elizabeth's attention to the radio. Her legs wobbled as she rose to her feet. Adrenaline still rushed through her arteries and soaked her muscles, but when she grasped the radio in her palm and squeezed the transmit button the words flowed unwavering from the computer scientist's mind to the receivers on the island.

The crew waited. In the distance a small speck of something smooth and reflective appeared above the horizon. On its exterior was a mirror image of the rocks and robots on the island below, then of the waves under it as it hovered across the water toward the humans. Elizabeth walked to the front of the flybridge to meet what she hoped would be a more agreeable representative of Singularity Island. Xavier stayed behind to keep the attacker within arm's reach. Sebastian sucked in a deep breath, readied his legs to handle all his weight, propped himself up with his good arm and expelled the breath with a grunt. He stood, his calves and quads screaming from the strain. Not much steadier on his feet than an infant, his legs buckled as gravity pulled him down, but he did not fall. Something firm and immobile held him upright. He turned to see the face of simulated benevolence displayed on Teresa's screen. Sebastian appreciated that she had foreseen his stumble well ahead of time and extended what remained of her hand to catch him. With renewed confidence he planted both feet on the deck, and together he and Teresa stood awaiting the oncoming drone.

A concave image of the boat and its passengers developed on the reflective underside of the hovering robot as it positioned itself over the flybridge. What the Singularity intended was made clear in the next moment. On the drone's outer casing the reflection of the rogue grew larger as the drone descended upon it. The Singularity bot had dropped itself so fast onto the rogue that it appeared accidental, but there was no crash nor crunching of polymer parts. Like a bird of prey the drone lifted its target off the floor and darted away in an instant. It carried the rogue to the starboard side where, unbeknownst to the crew, a large egg-shaped pod had been waiting in silence.

The pod was several meters of lustrous forest green. It

had no indentations. It had no protrusions. In fact the egg seemed to have no discernible parts of any kind. But on one of its poles, just visible under the waves splashing up against its outer shell, a dark gray tube was attached, one which extended from the pod all the way to the island, and the crew lost sight of the tube as it continued far beneath the undulating ocean surface.

Before the crewmates could process how long the pod had been lying in wait off their starboard bow, the top of the pod opened. The hovering drone dropped in the rogue bot and dashed back to the island. When the pod sealed up again, it receded back under water. A series of faint booming noises, not unlike thunder in the distance, reached the ears of Elizabeth. She also observed subtle vibrations in the tube, no doubt the disintegrated remnants of a recycled worker bot flowing back to the Singularity. Then the pod disappeared, and there was only ocean.

"Well that was creepy," said Teresa.

The humans on the flybridge stood mesmerized. A few days ago, life had been plodding along for them in the usual, predictable fashion. In a few passing days they had witnessed their town held hostage by technology, survived a series of attacks while others had not, confronted the most powerful force on Earth and pulled through at the cost of a few bandages. Elizabeth's insight, and the help of her trusted friends, had saved countless people in her hometown from experimentation, torture and death.

Sebastian, careful not to disturb his wounds lest another sensation of stabbing flood his body, turned to Elizabeth. "So what are you gonna tell the police?"

30

Elizabeth's eyes widened while the rest of her stiffened to an icicle. She cursed herself for neglecting such a pressing matter, even though it loomed over her through the better part of the voyage. Now the time had come to face her accusers. A part of her wanted to dismiss the detective's warning about not leaving town. Another part wanted to prostrate herself before the law and beg forgiveness, but as usual her rational side prevailed. "Teresa," she asked her lifelong companion, "tell me you got video footage of the attack."

Teresa rotated her black facial void toward Elizabeth. The artificial face appeared, smiled, and gave a wink. "Oh yes. My camera recorded until I was stabbed, then LiDAR and all other activity sensors took over." Elizabeth allowed herself an exhale of relief as Teresa continued. "I've already made a clip of composite footage using all the input. Would you like me to send it to the police or post it online?"

"Both," she said. "And make sure the police also get the code used by the rogue. Might be my only shot at forgiveness." The crew discussed Elizabeth's innocence a little further, halting only when Teresa jingled to make an announcement.

"Pardon the interruption," she said, "but you may want to turn your attention portside toward the north of the island." As was her programming and her custom, the bot made by Harmony pointed in the direction of interest to help the humans follow her verbal instructions.

At the foot of the north rock face, on a platform suspended and stationary amid the crashing waves, there stood a tower. To the far away crew it appeared no larger than a needle sticking straight up through a tea saucer, but given their distance from the island, this structure must have been truly enormous.

Sebastian asked Elizabeth, "Is that —"

"Yup," she answered. "That's the same launch pad."

A blinding flash erupted from the base of the needle and then disappeared just as quickly. The needle separated from the saucer, and it rose through the air as if in slow motion, reaching toward the heavens. "Teresa, TV display," requested Elizabeth, expecting the bot's camera to be on maximum zoom. All human eyes shifted back and forth from the live event to the live stream on Teresa's torso while the rocket pierced into the ever-thinning atmosphere, a darkening sky inviting the javelin into a soft, gentle, near zero gravity. When it moved beyond their visual range, the humans crowded around Teresa to watch the needle. The sliver of chrome diminished into a background of purple velvet, then it vanished.

It was only now, after the excitement had quieted and the waters had calmed, that a faraway voice, muffled and crackling through a megaphone, seeped into the ears of Elizabeth. After a moment she discovered the source. On the horizon was a vessel sitting just outside the island's restricted zone. The vessel bore a gathering of people, some of whom were clapping, but most of them stood, food or drink in hand, staring at the large screen on the deck. The screen was black but for a sprinkling of stars and the chrome javelin gliding past the flickering jewels. While some in the crowd continued their stargazing, others began to disperse and return to their cabin as the ferry rotated 180 degrees to return home.

Sebastian asked, "Think that's the same boat that brought you here a few days ago?"

Her eyes squinted. "Looks like the one I was just on. Same company for sure."

Xavier and his crewmates once more faced the island of machines. "The Singularity did it again," he remarked. "Whatcha think, Elizabeth? Is their launch heading for Jupiter this time?"

Elizabeth's auburn eyebrows twitched upward while her rosy lip protruded, as if to remind her friend the answer would be on the news by tomorrow.

Sebastian asked, "You think humans will ever get that far? Our physical performance is limited by cells and organs. Our understanding and imagination are limited by brain capacity. What purpose will humans serve in a universe where machines can outperform us at everything?"

Xavier shot him a quizzical glance. "If there were some alien race out there way more intelligent than humans, we'd still go on living our lives like we always have."

"Yeah, but look at what that Singularity has accomplished.

We know the ultimate goal of humanity is to populate other planets and eventually spread ourselves across the universe. But the machines have beaten us to the punch. They'll find our holy grail before we even get out the door to search for it. They've surpassed us in everything that matters. They've won the race."

"Don't you counsel patients on depression," Xavier asked. "Maybe you should just hand them the suicide weapon from now on."

Sebastian continued, stewing in his own pessimism. "I'm just saying, humans are like the old, decrepit nursing home residents, having raised the next generation to run the world while we sit in decay and wait for death." Xavier fought the urge to roll his eyes while Sebastian finished. "If anything we can do machines can do better, then why does anything we do matter?" The doctor's voice grew louder as his pitch elevated. It was almost comical, but his friends weren't sure he was joking. "To superintelligent machines, a human is the proverbial ant upon a leaf. How can dumb creatures like us possibly hope to remain of value to them?"

Elizabeth said, "An ant colony isn't trying to make itself valuable to us. Why should we care if we're valuable to the AI? We're valuable to each other. How else could we solve the biggest problems facing humanity? We form relationships to tackle life's challenges more easily, and because we believe our species has value, we will keep on living."

Xavier gave a nod. "Yeah, we don't care if the Singularity values us. We care about our own survival. Besides, we believe we matter to God. He made us in His image, so He has a vested interest in us."

"And we're valuable for our creativity," said Elizabeth. "What's more important than diversity of thought? Our emotions, our passions, our cultures and traditions let us experience the universe in a way machines never could."

Now Teresa chimed in with the accumulated wisdom of countless ancestors. "A child who graduated valedictorian from a school in the ghetto has accomplished no less than the highest graduate of Harvard. A gold medalist in the Special Olympics may have achieved more than the world's fastest or strongest man due to the many limitations he or she had to overcome. When humans attain their goals, it is always something to celebrate."

Sebastian took some shuffling steps, hobbling along until he reached the conn. The anchor reeled in; the boat rotated on its axis until it faced the mainland. As the crew began their long journey home, Sebastian asked, "You think humans will ever go beyond our solar system?"

"Maybe not in our lifetime," said Elizabeth. "But yes. I know we will."

A Note from the Author

If you enjoyed reading this, please leave a review on Amazon. I read every review and they help new readers discover my books.

For more updates, please sign up at https://authorcyeasted.com.

Acknowledgement

THANK YOU to the following:

EDITOR
Susan DiGirolamo, Esq.

And a SPECIAL THANKS to
Kurt Krizek
Thomas Doody
Joseph Gibes
JoEllen Yeasted
Gabriel Murillo Nader
All the loved ones of different professions who offered
their insights.

About the Author

Dr. Christian Yeasted is Chair of Ethics at St. Elizabeth Hospital. His research is in the ethics of artificial intelligence and how it relates to the future of humanity. While maintaining a clinical practice in Youngstown, OH, he also instructs medical students and residents in primary care, and his passion for teaching in ways that hold the learner's interest is apparent in The Final Invention.

9 798989 914807